MW01087530

HIDDEN IN PLAIN SIGHT, A SWEET ROMANTIC SUSPENSE

Forbidden Lake Romance, Book 1

ELANA JOHNSON

AEJ
CREATIVE WORKS

Copyright © 2022 by Elana Johnson

All rights reserved.

No part of this book may be reproduced in any form or by any electronic or mechanical means, including information storage and retrieval systems, without written permission from the author, except for the use of brief quotations in a book review.

ISBN-13: 978-1638760757

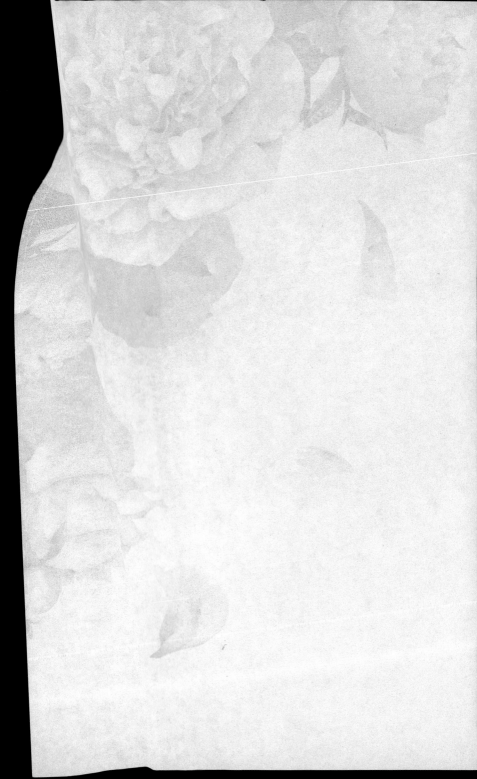

CHAPTER ONE

C assie Caldwell forced herself away from her desk off the instructional kitchen in the coldest building on the campus at Northwestern Michigan College. A new round of classes had begun that day, and she just had one more to make it through.

The practice kitchen, with its stainless steel workstations and industrial ovens, felt even chillier than her drab office. She set about putting the tools the students would be using that evening at each spot, thinking of who Thomas would be, or Katia, or Jonathan.

She loved her special needs course, and she only got one per semester. They brought a vibrancy to the kitchen that no other group could, and they always proved her point that anyone could learn to cook.

As she put a syllabus printed on goldenrod paper at each spot beside the hand soap, cinnamon, oil, and paring knife, a rush of gratitude for this job hit her. She'd only been at the university for a year, and this was only her third introductory culinary course for special needs students.

But she loved teaching her other four classes too, especially compared to waking up at two-thirty in the morning and heading to Donut Delight to make pastries for the five a.m. open time. No one in Forbidden Lake even came to the doughnut shop that early, but Addalyn Merchant—the closest thing to a best friend Cassie had allowed herself to have—insisted they open at the ungodly hour.

"Just in case," she said.

Cassie had only made the mistake of asking her "Just in case of what?" once. And she'd only worked at the shop for a week before she found out the answer. One Carlson Bixby.

Cassie could admit he was good-looking, with all his dark hair and those dreamy eyes. He wore a suit every day to his office in the city buildings, and he stopped by for coffee and a cherry fritter every Thursday morning.

So "just in case" was for Thursdays, and Addy's huge crush on the parks department director that claimed he'd be mayor one day.

Cassie shook her head as she placed the last paper at the last station. "Ninety minutes," she muttered to herself. If she could just get through the next ninety minutes, she could get home to Lars and Kyle, her twin half-brothers.

Fifteen was no joke for anyone, and her half-siblings had been through a lot in the past year and a half. A sharp pang of missing hit Cassie right behind her ribs, and she wondered if she'd ever be able to think about her mother without the accompanying pain in her chest.

Probably not.

She pressed against her side and went up to the front of the room, where a demo kitchen sat, an angular mirror above it so students could see what she was doing on the counter from anywhere in the room.

Her fantasies took over for a moment, and she closed her eyes as she imagined herself to be a celebrity chef, whisking something together in front of a camera. She opened her eyes and tilted the empty bowl toward the classroom, a picture-perfect smile on her face. "See how it comes together, but you haven't lost the air in the egg whites? That's what you want it to look like."

When she let go of it, the bowl made a clanging sound as the bottom of it hit the counter. She wasn't going to be a celebrity chef. Then the twins' father would know where she was. Where his sons were.

And Cassie could absolutely not allow that.

She pulled her phone out, her anxiety suddenly boiling over. It was Larry Glassman's parole hearing today, and Cassie still had a few friends in Chicago she could rely on. Willie Ashford was one, but the cute stylist Cassie had gone to for years hadn't texted yet. Maybe Larry's parole had been denied.

Hope floated behind Cassie's heart, but she never let it stay for long. She'd gotten legal guardianship and custody of Lars and Kyle after their mother had died fifteen months ago. They'd immediately had a family council and decided to leave Chicago.

Five hours north, they'd stopped in the quaint lakeside town—and cherry capital of the nation—of Forbidden Lake. She'd gotten the job at the bakery, and then the university, and Cassie was doing the best she could to keep them all safe, secret, and together.

The door at the back of the room opened, and her first student peered inside. "Welcome," she said in a falsely bright voice, though class didn't start for another fifteen minutes. Her special needs students often came very early, as some of them had trouble with directions or finding their classrooms.

"Is this introductory cooking?" the man asked, his words a bit thick.

"Yes," she said. "You can choose any station."

"I'm Drew," he said, entering the room. An older woman

—clearly his mother—came in behind him "And this is my mom, Ruthann."

"Hello," Cassie said. "I'm Cassandra Caldwell. I'll be your professor." She shook hands with Drew and his mother, who then promptly left. As the minutes ticked by, Cassie met all but one of her students, and they'd all chosen a station.

The clock ticked to five, and she strode to the front of the room, saying, "All right, it's time to begin. Let's start with the roll. Let me know you're here when I call your name." She went down the list, trying to memorize the name that went with each face as the students indicated they were here.

"So we're missing Jonathan Addler," she said, glancing around. At that moment, the door in the back opened again, and a man stepped inside.

He clearly did not have special needs, unless drop-dead gorgeous made the list of handicaps one might suffer from. And he definitely wasn't suffering.

He wore a crisp pair of jeans and a polo the color the cherries would be in the summer. His dark hair swooped to the side like he'd just gotten off the set of an action movie where he rode a motorcycle along the beach.

There was a beach here, so maybe he had.

Cassie's heart pinged around inside her chest, and she didn't even know why. She'd met good-looking men before. Dated a few. Kissed a couple.

He ran his hand down his face, where he wore a neatly trimmed beard, as he glanced around and then to her. "Here," he said, an arrogant smile curving his mouth.

Wow, what a mouth.

Cassie tore her gaze from his lips and cleared her throat. "Jonathan Addler?" she asked.

He strode over to the only empty station and sat on the stool like everyone else, his smile moving from arrogance to curiosity the longer she stared at him. He really was going to stay. She glanced around at the other students. Half of them were looking at her, and the other half were watching Jonathan.

She put her clipboard down and cocked her head toward the office door to her left. "Can I speak with you for a moment?"

"Am I in trouble already?" he asked. "I was five minutes late."

"Now," she said, marching over to her office and waiting for him to enter in front of her. Closing herself in a tighter space with this delicious male specimen wasn't her greatest idea. Or maybe it was. She wasn't exactly thinking straight at the moment. Not with all that pine tree, musky goodness now filling her nose.

The door clicked closed behind her, and Cassie wondered what in the blazes she was doing. Hadn't another professor just been fired for having a relationship with a student?

Yes! her mind screamed. *Open the door!*

But she couldn't have this conversation with him in front of the other students. She cracked the door and glanced over her shoulder. With the large window, she could see several other students, which meant they could see her too.

"This is a special needs course, Jonathan," she said as quietly as she could.

"Jon," he said.

She blinked and employed her patience. "Okay. *Jon*. This is a special needs course. For students with special needs."

"I have a special need," he said.

She folded her arms. "You do?"

"Yeah, I *need* to take this class."

Annoyance surged through her at the same time desire made her head swim. She had some needs too, but that didn't mean she did whatever she wanted. He couldn't either.

"Well, you don't have a mental disability," she said. "This

course is for students with mental disabilities. It will be rather slow and dull for someone like you." She let her eyes wander down the length of his body and back.

When her gaze met his again, she realized she'd given away too much.

"Someone like me?" he asked, his dark eyes flashing dangerously.

A thrill ran through her, but she tamped it down. She could not start a relationship with a student. Oh, no. She could not. She needed this job if she ever wanted to sleep through the night again. Number two, she wasn't dating anyone until the twins were adults and on their own. She'd promised her mother she'd make sure Lars and Kyle were taken care of until then. Safe from Larry. Prepared for the world.

And that meant she didn't have time to be flirting or dating or building a relationship with a guy.

"You'll have to transfer out," she said, her voice not quite as strong as she'd like it to be.

"The other sections are all full."

"So you thought you could just sign up for this one?"

"I just registered last week. I'm not taking anyone's spot."

"You don't know that." She shook her head, doubt trickling through her. Had Larry sent someone to see if she was the Cassandra Caldwell that had his sons?

Don't be ridiculous, she told herself. She hadn't even heard if he was out on parole yet. He had no idea where they were. But Jon still couldn't stay in the class. Her supervisor had only allowed this class after Cassie had promised to only take special needs students in it.

"Sorry, Mister Addler." She twisted the knob behind her though the door was already cracked and stepped into the kitchen.

"All right, guys," she said, finding her thoughts on what

CHAPTER TWO

Jonathan Addler was staying in this introductory culinary arts class, thank you very much. It didn't matter that the instructor had told him to get out. Transfer.

He almost scoffed.

She was a fiery little thing, he'd give her that. But Jon was determined to learn to cook, so Marcy Winston would go out with him.

After all, he was a master carpenter—very good with his hands. How hard could cooking be?

He rubbed himself down with the oil, just as Cassandra Caldwell instructed him to. Then he sprinkled cinnamon in his palms and spread that around too. He had no idea what her point was, but everyone else was going along with her too.

"Hand-washing is the most important thing we do in the kitchen," she said, and the lightbulb went off in Jon's head. "Think of all those brown spots of cinnamon as germs. Germs make people sick."

She spoke in a slow, clear voice, but she wasn't patronizing the other students in the class.

"We have to get all the germs off before we cook," she said. "So now, I want row one to go over to the sinks on the left and wash in cold water. I want row two over here on the right to wash in hot water. And I want row three at the sinks in the back to take their soap with them, and use hot water."

Jon grabbed his bottle of soap, glad that he was on the back row. With the scent of cinnamon thick in the air, he couldn't smell Cassandra's orange-honey skin anymore, and he actually mourned the loss of it.

He almost tripped when he realized what he'd just thought. Cutting a glance at the professor, he could admit she was pretty. Beautiful even. With long, straight hair the color of midnight, and curves he wouldn't want anywhere in his construction plans. Oh, no. Those were all made of straight lines and right angles.

Heat started in his toes and moved upward, and Jon wondered what in the world was happening. He'd had a crush on Marcy for six months. Six solid months, and she wouldn't go out with him. Finally, in a desperate move he only sort of regretted, he'd asked her what it would take.

"I've always wanted a man who could cook," she'd said. A giggle and a flip of her blonde hair followed, and Jon had signed up for this class that evening.

But now, looking at Cassandra....

"Your turn," someone said, and he jerked his attention away from the teacher. He scrubbed good and hard at his hands, making the water as hot as he could stand, and even adding more soap to make sure he got everything.

"Time's up," Cassandra called just as he finished. Someone handed him a towel, and he dried his hands. "Let's see. Everyone here in the middle. Cold water group, show us first."

He joined the other eleven students and saw that cold water had basically done nothing to remove the "germs" from their hands. Even hot water hadn't done the job. And everyone in his group except for him still had cinnamon on their hands in some places.

Cassandra scowled at him when she saw his impeccably clean hands. She latched onto his wrist and held up his hand. "How did you do that?" she asked, almost like an accusation.

"Lots of soap," he said. "Lots of scrubbing." Sparks tingled down his arm, originating from the spot where her skin met his. He swallowed, finding it harder than normal to do so.

"Okay, guys," she said. "Hot water. Lots of soap. Lots of scrubbing." She dropped his hand with a disgusted look. "Go get all those germs off and meet back here."

Jon had taken one step when she said, "You stay here, Mister Addler. You're already clean."

Instead of sinking, Jon's heart bounced around inside his chest as he turned back to Cassandra. "I didn't mean to ruin your lesson. Have you ever had oil and cinnamon all over your hands?" He didn't like it.

"I'm getting the transfer paper now," she said, heading back to her office.

"Don't do that," he said, following her with long strides. He caught her just as she reached the door. "I'll stay out of the way. You won't even know I'm here." He put his hand against the door frame so she'd have to duck to get into her office. He smiled at her, one of the grins his sisters said he used on their mother to get his way.

Whether that was true or not, it did melt a little of the ice in Cassandra's eyes.

"Let's make a deal," he said quickly before she could kick him out for good. "You let me take this class, and I'll build you whatever you want."

Her eyebrows went up. "What?"

"I'm a carpenter. Best one in town, if I do say so myself."
But he didn't have to. Addler Construction—his firm—had
won Best in County awards for five years now. "I'll build you
something. A dresser. A deck, even. Nothing as big as a
house. But something."

She folded her arms again, and dang if that wasn't a sexy
little move. She probably didn't understand how it made his
blood run hotter and his throat drier.

And Jon's focus for why he wanted to be in this class
shifted, and shifted hard. Away from Marcy.

Toward Cassandra.

And he knew if she agreed to his little deal, he was going
to be in so much trouble.

The silence between them lengthened, and Jon felt sure
she had experience in glaring down someone.

"I have great hands," he said.

She scoffed. "Is that a pick-up line?"

"No," he said, wondering why her reluctance to have him
in her class was revving him up so much.

"Fine," she finally said, falling back a step. "You can stay in
the class. And I'll need to see evidence of your 'great hands'
before I decide if I want you to build me something."

"Fair enough," Jon said, sure she'd love anything he
showed her. "I'm sure you'll like what you see."

Her eyes drifted down to his feet and back again, and
Jon felt like she already liked what she saw. He kept his
expression impassive, though, and watched as her face
colored and she nodded before turning back to the class. "All
right, guys. When you're finished, come on back to your
stations."

Jon had never had any problems getting a date—until
Marcy Winston, of course. And that had driven him to a near
obsession with the woman. But as he listened to Cassandra
talk about holding a knife and using a rocking motion to slice,

he couldn't help thinking that Marcy had gotten things right —cooking definitely was sexy.

He shook his head to clear it. He didn't want to lose a fingertip tonight, because he was already on shaky ground with Cassandra. He made it through the lesson and put together a pretty good salad if he did say so himself.

Of course he didn't. He congratulated the man next to him on his knife cuts and gave Colton a high-five before they dug into their greens. Jon barely ate any of his, as he was more of a meat and potatoes kind of guy.

Cassandra stood at the door after the kitchen had been cleaned up, and she smiled and said good-bye to every person. She'd remembered all of their names after only one class period, and dang if that little detail didn't make Jon's internal temperature shoot toward the sky—which was a good thing, as it was chest-numbingly cold outside in Michigan in January.

"Good night, Jon," she said curtly, the smile fading from that pretty face.

"Can I get your number?" he asked boldly, only feeling the slightest tremor behind his lungs. "Then I can text you some pictures of my handiwork."

She blinked those long lashes at him, and he definitely saw something fearful in her eyes. "Give me yours, and I'll text you."

"What difference does it make?" he asked. "I'll still have your number."

"I—" She swallowed—definitely afraid of something—and a mask slid over her face, concealing her emotions from him. But Jon had three sisters, and he recognized female panic when he saw it.

"I'm a nice guy," he said gently. Maybe his stature intimidated her. Maybe he shouldn't have been so forward. "My family owns the Sunshine Shores Cherry Orchards and

Resort on the east side of the lake. Maybe you'd like to come out there and I don't know." Why was Jon still talking? He drew in a deep breath, expanding his lungs to full capacity. "Get away for a night or two. The cabins don't fill up in the winter."

She softened a bit, and Jon wanted to smile encouragingly at her. He kept his mask in place too, though. "Thank you," she said. "But I can't. I work at the bakery in the morning, and I don't need to get up any earlier than I have to."

"Ah, got it." It was a ten-minute drive out to the orchards. "All right, well, I'll give you my number."

"You can have mine." She rattled it off before Jon could so much as swipe on his phone, so she had to repeat it once he got to his contacts.

He did smile at her then, and when her lips curved up too, the whole room got brighter. Or maybe that was Jon's imagination. No matter what, he left campus that night thinking he could've just made the best decision of his life—or the worst.

"PHOENIX?" HE CALLED AS HE OPENED THE DOOR TO HIS brother's remote cabin. The house wasn't really that remote, but it was crowded by cherry trees and wild land the family hadn't cultivated yet on the north, and the state forest on the south. From Jon's house closer to the road and the rest of the family, it was a fifteen-minute walk. And in sub-zero temperatures?

Yeah, Jon had driven an ATV.

His younger brother turned from the stove, and with Phoenix wearing an apron over his lumberjack-type clothes, Jon would've never found him intimidating. "Hey," he said. "I'm making Adam and Eve on a raft. You want one?"

Fried eggs and toast? "Yes, please," Jon said, entering the cabin and closing the door behind him. Phoenix had a fire roaring in the pot-bellied stove, and that heated the small space just fine.

Jon held his hands over the black stove for a moment as he asked, "Am I intimidating?"

Phoenix cracked an egg into the pan, which sizzled upon contact. "Intimidating?"

"Yeah, this woman looked at me tonight, and I think she was scared."

"Oh, boy." Phoenix focused on his cooking. He wasn't exactly a recluse. He came into the family lodge for parties and dinners and gatherings. But he definitely liked his privacy, and he was the only sibling that lived away from the family block of cabins in the southern end of the orchards.

"Oh boy what?" Jon asked.

"Another woman?" Phoenix gave him a look that said way more than those two words.

"I haven't been out with anyone in months," Jon said, a definite note of defense in his tone.

"That's because Marcy won't go out with you."

"This isn't Marcy."

Phoenix flipped the piece of toast with an egg in the middle, and Jon's mouth watered. "That makes it worse, bro, not better."

"Why? You don't date at all."

Phoenix's jaw tightened, and Jon regretted the words. He and Phoenix had been close since his brother's dirt bike accident in their teen years, so though another brother sat between them, when Jon needed advice, he didn't go to Liam. He always came out to this cabin and Phoenix.

"Who is it?" Phoenix asked.

"You don't know her." Phoenix never went to town. Well, almost never. He had his groceries delivered, and he didn't own a car. No need to stop by the gas station or do any shopping. He claimed to have the Internet out here, and he could buy anything with that.

In fact, Jon remembered his mother had given him a couple of packages for Phoenix. "Mom gave me some stuff for you." He backtracked toward the door.

"Don't think you can just walk out on the conversation," Phoenix said as Jon opened the door.

Jon looked over his shoulder. "She's my culinary arts professor."

"Oh, boy," Phoenix said again, this time bright curiosity in his eyes as he looked at Jon from across the cabin. "I can't wait to hear about that."

Jon ducked outside to the ATV to grab the packages, wondering if he should just shut up and enjoy his eggs. But his mind kept going back to Cassandra over and over again. He hadn't texted her yet, and he quickly pulled out his phone.

With numb fingers, he typed out, *Hey Cassandra. This is Jon from your class. Maybe we should meet so I can show you my work.*

He grinned at the glowing cell phone screen. Oh, yeah, he definitely wanted to see her again before Thursday's class. Wanted to see her every day. Find out what hid behind those beautiful eyes, and if she was scared of him or just anxious in general. Something male and overbearing roared within him, and he felt the need to protect her from whatever plagued her.

Even if it's you? his mind whispered.

He ignored that thought, sent the text, and got the heck out of the cold before he froze to death thinking about the beautiful brunette who'd suddenly come into his life.

CHAPTER THREE

Cassie stared at her phone, a little surprised Jon had texted already. She'd been expecting him to, sure. But not tonight. He'd worked so easily in the kitchen, she'd been able to tell he had great hands.

"Great hands," she muttered to herself, wishing her mind didn't take her down forbidden paths with the words.

Kyle sat on the other end of the couch, and he either didn't hear her or didn't care that she was talking to herself again. Lars had put a science fiction movie on the TV, and he lounged in the bean bag in front of them.

Maybe we should meet.

Cassie stared at those words, seemingly unable to look anywhere else. She felt warm and woozy, but that had to be from the all-meat pizza Lars had made. Didn't it?

She had to respond to Jon. Tell him absolutely that she couldn't meet him. That he couldn't even stay in the class. Dr. Langstrom had been clear. The special needs class was only for those with special needs.

And whatever Jon's was wouldn't qualify, Cassie knew that.

She had seen him help Colton a couple of times tonight, and an idea cracked through her like lightning.

Jon could be her assistant.

Then he wouldn't be a student.

But dating co-workers had also become frowned upon recently, what with the scandal that had just been settled at Northwestern Michigan College. No matter which way Cassie turned, starting a relationship with Jon couldn't happen.

Cassie, she typed out and sent. She didn't need him calling her by her full name. That was okay, wasn't it? She'd told her other culinary classes to call her Cassie. She'd been so flustered by Jon's sudden appearance in the wrong class, that she hadn't told them.

Her phone lit up with several texts, and she read Jon's first. *Okay, Cassie. Maybe we should meet so I can show you my stuff. I have some great photos printed.*

She'd also gotten one from Theresa Kim, her next-door neighbor who helped with the twins sometimes when Cassie's jobs kept her from getting home on time.

Your garage is still open. Just thought you'd want to know.

Cassie did want to know. A flicker of fear traveled through her, and she got up to go close the garage. She was always so careful to keep everything locked. Everything out of sight.

Thanks, she tapped out as she bumped the button to close the garage. A glance out into the night amped up her panic, and she worked to stamp it back down. Larry wasn't here. He hadn't seen her car in the garage. Everything was fine.

She checked the front door to make sure it was locked, and she scooped her tiny yorkie into her arms, hoping to steal some comfort from him. "Hey, Button," she whispered to the dog. "We're okay, right?"

The little dog yapped and yapped whenever anyone came

near the house, and he hadn't made a peep that night. So they really were fine.

Her blood chilled when she saw the last text was from her friend in Chicago. Willie had texted just three words: *He got out.*

Cassie took a breath, trying to convince herself not to pack everything they could and get out of the house that night.

Larry Glassman doesn't know where you are, she told herself. In fact, he wouldn't even know his sons had left the city until he met with his parole officer. Her mother's dying request had fallen on sympathetic ears, and the judge had deemed the custody and guardianship hearings and results sealed until Larry was released on parole.

And it had been fifteen months. Their trail was completely cold in Chicago, Cassie had made sure of that. The boys had gotten new phones so they couldn't text old friends, new haircuts so they wouldn't be recognized, new lives here in Forbidden Lake. They even went by her last name now and attended a charter school that kept all the doors locked while classes were in session.

Larry would not get to them.

She turned back to the living room, where Kyle and Lars still watched TV. She had to tell them about their dad, and her heart pounded at the thought. She'd have to be the strong one. The one to reassure them they'd get to stay with her. That Larry would never track them down.

Kyle would handle it better than Lars, and Cassie said, "Hey, guys, we need to talk for a minute. Can we pause the movie?"

Lars picked up the remote and stilled the frame, leaving Cassie no choice but to plow forward. She sat back in her spot, perched on the edge of the couch now, and handed Button to Lars. "Your dad was up for parole today."

Lars sucked in a breath and looked at Kyle. The pair of them were something to behold, identical right down to the worry in their dark eyes and the splash of freckles across their cheeks. Kyle wore his pitch-black hair a little longer, and he brushed nervously at the ends of it now.

Lars looked back at her. "He got out, didn't he?"

"Yes," she said. "He got out on parole. But it's okay." She tried a smile, but it was shaky and all wrong. "He can't leave the city for six months, I know that. Mom requested that he be required to stay there for six months after he got parole."

Lars got out of the bean bag, adjusting the little dog in his arms. "So we'll go somewhere else once school ends." He looked like he'd go pack right now.

Surprise tugged through Cassie. "You want to move?"

"You don't?" Lars exchanged a glance with Kyle.

"He has no idea where we are," Cassie said.

"And six months to question everyone in Chicago," Kyle said, his voice much quieter and less panicked than his twin's.

Cassie's nerves rioted. She'd been building a life for them here in Forbidden Lake. Gotten them into a good school. Had a good thing going at the university—which she hadn't told them about. "I'm up for a full-time professorship at the university," she said. "This would be huge for us. More money. I could quit at the bakery so I wouldn't have to be gone in the mornings."

There was so much she hadn't told them. "I don't think he'll find us. I left a few breadcrumbs that will take him thousands of miles away."

Kyle narrowed his eyes at her. "Like what?"

Her phone chimed again, and Willie had said, *Let me know if you need anything else. Erasing everything now.*

Thank you, Cassie typed out quickly. *I'm erasing too.* She looked up at her brothers. "Like, I put an announcement out that I'd gotten married. New last name. New adventure in

Europe. Neither of you were mentioned. Mom asked a friend to put your names in the foster care system. Split you up."

Cassie exhaled heavily, wondering if they'd feel betrayed that she hadn't told them about these safety measures before.

"So I don't think he'll find us. Ever. We'll be okay." And while she had urges to leave Forbidden Lake too, she also wanted to stay.

Jon's face flashed through her mind, but she pushed it away. She wasn't staying for him. She barely knew him. Just because he was the first man to accelerate her pulse in years didn't mean she'd risk her safety and the safety of her brothers to be with him.

Her phone chimed again, another text from Jon. *Sorry if this is too bold*, he'd said. Nothing else. She frowned, wondering what was too bold. Asking her to meet him? Then another message came in.

I just felt something between us, and I'd love to go out with you.

Her heart full-on stopped then, and she lost all track of her thoughts. She wasn't even aware Kyle had leaned over and was reading her texts until he said, "Who's asking you out?"

She flipped her phone over and kept it face-down on her lap, her heart beat racing as quickly as her mind.

"No one." She looked at the twins. "Let's think about what we really want, okay? We can have a family council in the morning when I get home from the bakery." She stood up and collected Button from Lars. "Pros, cons, worries, fears, all of it."

Her blasted phone chimed again and then again, and she knew they'd both be from Jon. Instead of looking at the messages, she shoved her phone in her back pocket and said, "I'm headed to bed. Two-thirty is only a few hours away." She pressed a kiss to Kyle's forehead and then Lars's.

"I love you guys," she said. "Nothing bad is going to happen to us, okay?"

Kyle nodded, but Lars looked like he'd just found out he'd swallowed poison. "Can I sleep in your room?" he asked.

"Sure," she said. "Grab the bean bag and bring it in."

"Me too?" Kyle asked, and Cassie wondered what she'd done to make these two teenagers think she and a tiny yorkie could protect them. Somehow, somewhere along the way, she had given them that message. And she wouldn't fail them.

So she said, "Of course. You have the futon under your bed, right?"

The next several minutes were filled with activity as they all got ready for bed. She let Button out and made sure all the doors and windows were locked before closing them all in the bedroom and locking that door too.

Kyle lay on the futon, and Lars seemed comfy curled up in the bean bag. She gave Button to him, and the little dog circled on his chest before lying down.

"Night, guys," she said, her brain full and exhaustion almost overpowering her. She got in bed too and turned her back away from the twins so she could finally check Jon's messages. Even as she told herself that she couldn't afford any distractions right now, her chest warmed at the sight of his texts.

Do you work at Donut Delight or Winners Eat Breakfast?

The fact that there were only two choices reminded Cassie of how small Forbidden Lake was.

I'm really feeling famished for doughnuts and coffee, Jon's last text read. *Maybe I'll see you in the morning.*

Cassie smiled despite the unrest building in her stomach. She typed out one word before silencing her phone and placing it face-down on her nightstand.

Maybe.

CHAPTER FOUR

J on tried to make it look like he was just walking down the street in front of the Donut Delight, but it was freaking cold and no human should be out at this ungodly hour. And yet he was.

Which showed everyone awake to see him that he was completely whipped by the culinary arts professor—including said professor standing behind the pastry counter in the cheerily lit bakery.

He saw her through the window, his thoughts switching from *Why do I live here? It's too dang cold* to *Wow, she's gorgeous.*

A smile graced her face as the bell rang and he entered the shop. Cassie leaned her hip into the counter, exchanged a glance with a blonde woman, who promptly went through the door into the back of the bakery.

"You made it," Cassie said, placing a to-go cup of coffee on the counter as if she'd had it ready for hours. Maybe she had. He'd gone to Winners Eat Breakfast first, and she hadn't been there.

He lifted the matted pictures he'd brought with him

under the pretenses of calling this a business meeting. Cassie hadn't exactly told him she wouldn't meet him. But she certainly hadn't said yes either.

"I was just walking by," he said, which made her shake her head and laugh lightly. He got the distinct impression she didn't laugh much, and Jon wanted to change that. To keep himself from blurting out such preposterous things, he peered into the dessert cases. "What's good here?"

"Everything's good here," she said. "I make it all."

"So one of everything then." He looked at her, noticing the surprise mingling with pure desire in her eyes. He'd lost some sleep last night after her text, wondering if maybe —*maybe*—the spark between them had only been on his end.

But looking into the dark depths of her eyes, he knew it wasn't.

She started plucking one pastry from every tray, and Jon laughed. "Wait, maybe I want to change my mind."

"Nope," she said. "We have a strict no-mind-changing policy here at Donut Delight." She flashed him a smile made purely of flirt. "You can take them back to the orchard." He leaned into the counter and watched her work. He'd always found the simplest of things alluring, and she wore a dark apron smudged with frostings and flour. Her dedication to this job showed in her early arrival every morning, and Jon's attraction flared again.

"Have you been digging up information on me and my family?" he asked.

"Heavens, no," she said, placing the last pastry in the third box and putting a lid on it. She looked at him, and the moment stretched. "My night was full of homework and sci-fi movies." Her chin lifted as if she dared him to freak out and walk away.

"You have kids," he said, pulling his wallet out of his back pocket, glad when the words didn't pitch up into a question at the end.

"One hundred and twelve dollars, and thirty-four cents." She took his card, ran it through the machine, and added, "I've never been pregnant, but I do take care of my two fifteen-year-old half-brothers."

"Full time?" Jon asked. "By yourself?"

Her eyes flashed with dangerous fire, and dang if Jon didn't want to get burned by her. Repeatedly. "Yes." She ripped off his receipt and handed it to him with his card. "The coffee's on me. Thanks for coming by, Mister Addler."

He blinked, his hand still extended toward her, the card barely balancing between two fingers. "Mister Addler?" He moved then, stuffing his card back into its slot in his wallet. "I thought we were past that."

Even though she looked very much like she was interested, she shook her head. "I don't date students," she said.

"I'm not really a student," he said. "I'm barely part-time, and I didn't go last semester at all."

"Why did you sign up now then?"

Ah, of course she'd ask that. Jon sighed and reached for the boxes of pastries. "So you don't want to even look at my work?"

"You said you had a special need."

"You're pushy," he said.

"*You're* the one who wouldn't leave *my* class last night," she shot back. "You were so desperate to stay, you made me a deal." She nodded toward the pictures still clenched under his arm, as if he hadn't been present for any of their earlier encounters.

"I *offered* the deal," he clarified. "You still haven't taken it."

"Fine." She swept her hand toward the empty doughnut shop. "Let's have a look at those pictures." She moved from behind the counter, and Jon felt very much like a satellite. She was the sun, and he'd rotate around her forever.

He tried to push the feelings and thoughts away, bury them deep, but they surged against his attempts. She pressed into his personal space to get the boxes, and he didn't give her an inch of breathing room.

Their eyes met, and time stopped. Oh, yeah, Jon would be kissing this woman. Soon. The craving to do so almost clouded his rational thoughts completely, causing the male instinct within him to take over.

And in his opinion, if she didn't date students, even better. "I can keep a secret," he said, causing time to flow forward again. She collected the pastry boxes and started walking over to a table in the corner.

He snatched the coffee and followed her, wondering if she was consciously adding an extra sway to her hips. No matter what, she drove his desire for her to the edge of insanity, and she probably didn't even know it.

She sat facing the entirety of the shop, and he noticed the way her gaze swept the space, lingering on the door. That inkling of fear resided in her expression for a moment, and then she focused on him.

"There's no secrets to keep," she said.

"But we could." He sat on the chair opposite of her. "I meant what I said last night."

Her eyes glittered like dark diamonds, and she opened one of the boxes and took out a long maple bar. "We wouldn't be able to go out in public."

"My family owns thousands of acres of cherry orchards."

"It's January."

"We have thirty cabins." Jon was certain he could find a solution to anything she said.

Interest sparked in her eyes as she took a slow bite of her

doughnut. Jon tracked the movement, licking his own lips as she cleaned the frosting from hers.

"Anyway," she said. "I was thinking of talking to my boss about hiring you as an assistant. But I still don't date co-workers."

"Again, I'm a pro secret-keeper. I have five brothers and sisters. We were always keeping secrets from my parents—and each other."

"I suppose that's a pretty good résumé."

Victory shot through Jon, and he too reached for a pastry. He didn't even care what it was. He barely glanced at the cinnamon roll before taking a bite of it. Big mistake. The soft, squishy, disgusting raisin mushed between his teeth.

"Ugh." He scrambled for a napkin and spit the offending food into it, wiping his mouth carefully before looking at Cassie.

She burst out laughing, and again, Jon felt sure she had no idea what that sound did to his insides. They vibrated and laughed with her, hoping they could make such a happy sound come from her again. Soon. So soon.

"Who puts raisins in a perfectly good cinnamon roll?" he asked, poking at the pastry. "There should be a warning label."

"I like them with raisins," she said, picking up his treat and taking a bite of it. "And nuts."

"No." He shook his head. "Now you're just trying to be difficult."

She lifted one slim shoulder into a shrug. "Why'd you sign up for my class?" She put the cinnamon roll back in front of him, and he glanced at it. He wasn't going to eat it, but he sure wanted to have his mouth where hers had been.

What he really wanted was to touch his mouth to hers right now. Instead, he reached across the table and brushed a piece of hair off her forehead that had fallen there. She froze, her eyes wide, and he smiled softly at her. This was the smile Phoenix had told him to use, the one he gave to their sisters on their birthdays.

While he wasn't remotely interested in Cassie as just a friend, he definitely wanted her as a girlfriend. And to do that, he had to be friendly.

"Promise not to laugh?" he asked.

"I can't promise that."

"I suppose not." He looked back to the pastry counter, but the blonde woman had disappeared. He heaved a sigh, like this information was costing him a great deal. Because it was. He didn't think Cassie would go out with him after he told her.

She's not going out with you now, he told himself. Unless he could get her to agree to be his secret lover, he'd have to settle for seeing her in class.

"I signed up, because there's a woman I was interested in," he said. "And she said she wouldn't go out with me unless I knew how to cook." There was another reason, but he wouldn't have chosen Introduction to Culinary Arts for his last elective if Marcy hadn't said she wanted a man who could cook.

Cassie gave him one, two, three heartbeats of silence before she snorted and then sure enough—laughed. "And now you're asking me out." She covered her partially eaten maple bar with her napkin. "You're a piece of work, Mister Addler."

"Jon," he corrected again. He placed the pictures on the table. "I have to get to work, but I'll leave these with you." He plucked a business card from his coat pocket and laid it on top of the mounted pictures of his parents' anniversary dresser and the kitchen table and chairs where he'd won Best in State at a furniture showing two years ago.

"My card has my website and business number. If you like what you see...." He stood up and leaned over the table toward her, brushing that hair out of her face again. "And I'm sure you will. That you already do. Call me. Like I said, I'm *really* good at keeping secrets."

And while he wanted to stay and taste that frosting again, only this time from her lips, he turned and walked calmly out of the bakery.

CHAPTER FIVE

Cassie stood nervously outside Dr. Langstrom's office, her fingers braiding themselves together and pulling apart almost like they had brains of their own. She was stupid. Stupid for requesting this meeting. Stupid for thinking she could get out of it now without a big explanation. Stupid for even *thinking* about going out with Jonathan Addler.

Even as her aide, assistant, helper, whatever, he'd become an employee of the university, and the relationship would still be forbidden.

She turned to leave—she could text something about one of the twins needing her—just as the door opened. "Come on in, Cassie," Dr. Langstrom said, her voice pleasant.

Cassie fixed a smile on her face before turning back to her boss. Sure, Dr. Langstrom might look pleasant, but there really wasn't a happy bone in the woman's body. Almost sixty, she'd worked in education for almost forty years now, and her keen eyes missed nothing.

Not the way Cassie straightened her clothes before

marching toward her. Not the way she twisted her fingers together one last time as she entered the office.

Dr. Langstrom was no-nonsense, right down to her stylish pixie haircut and precise gold hoops in her ears. Cassie had never seen her in anything but a pantsuit or a skirt suit, and today was no exception.

She settled in front of the desk and waited for Dr. Langstrom to go around to the other side. "What brings you here today?" she asked.

Nerves fluttered through her with the strength of a flock of birds being frightened into the sky. She opened her mouth to speak, but nothing came out.

"If it's about the full-time position," Dr. Langstrom started.

"It's not," Cassie said. "My special needs class is full, and I'm wondering if we have the budget to hire an aide." There, she'd said it.

Dr. Langstrom frowned and leaned back in her chair. Her nose was a bit hooked, almost like an eagle, and she certainly struck fear right between all of Cassie's ribs when her eyebrows pulled down into a V. "An aide? You've run full classes before without help."

"There are some particularly difficult students in this group." Cassie tasted the lie on her tongue as the words left her mouth. What in the world was she doing? Her life felt crowded with questions now, and she didn't have the answers for any of them.

I'm really good at keeping secrets.

She'd had no doubt about Jon's ability to do anything he said he could. Especially after she'd looked through the pictures he'd left with her. The man had not lied about his extreme talent with his hands, and Cassie had only been able to think about what other magic the man could do with those fingers in the twelve hours since he'd left the bakery.

She'd also been toying with renting one of his cabins for a while. Just to get away from the house in case Larry came looking.

Which was stupid, as Larry himself couldn't actually come looking.

"Well, I'm afraid I don't have the budget," Dr. Langstrom said.

"I understand," Cassie said, standing. She'd taken a couple of steps toward the door, almost desperate to get out of this stuffy office, when she turned back. "And I do hope I'm still being considered for the full-time position."

"Of course." Dr. Langstrom smiled at her, but it was made of pure politics. Cassy had seen those kinds of smiles before, and they annoyed her instantly. But she smiled too and let herself out of the office.

So that was that. Jon couldn't become her co-worker. He'd stay her student. She could be professional; she always had been before.

She needed this job—needed the full-time position if she had any hope of a more normal life with Kyle and Lars.

So she'd see Jon on Tuesdays and Thursdays from five to six-thirty, same as the other special needs students.

If only she could stop thinking about what it would be like to kiss him.

THURSDAY AT FIVE O'CLOCK SNUCK UP ON HER LIKE A THIEF in the night. Before she knew it, Jon walked through the door, looking delicious enough to eat and class hadn't even started yet.

She liked that he had a big family, that he seemed fond of them and worked with them around the orchards. She had refused to allow herself even a moment to look up his carpentry business and learn more about him that way.

The fact that he ran his own business impressed her, and she wondered if she could perhaps perpetuate their relationship by hiring him. Or asking him to help her with a business consultation. After all, she did want to start her own restaurant someday, and he obviously ran a successful enterprise.

They weren't alone in the kitchen, but the tether between them made everyone else fall away. She nodded to him, but he came right up to her. "Well? Did you look at the designs?"

"I did," she said.

"And?"

She glared at him, quite unsure why she couldn't just kick him out of her mental space. But flirting with him had been fun. The heat from his touch, light as it had been against her skin, had ignited a fire inside her that she'd thought had gone cold long ago.

"I'd like to request another meeting," she said as aloofly as possible. "We can discuss the terms then."

"Intriguing." He grinned at her and went to the back of the room, where he immediately engaged in a conversation with Colton, his table-mate. He didn't look at her more than necessary, and he put together a perfectly seared chicken dish as instructed. He left with the other students without a backward glance, and Cassie actually felt neglected by him.

Once home, she put together the same chicken dish she'd just taught to her students, fed the twins, and asked them about homework. The evening was as normal as it ever had been since they'd come to Forbidden Lake—except for her ever-present thoughts of Jon.

What would Kyle and Lars think of her dating a man? She'd never done it since she'd gotten guardianship of them. She'd wanted them to know and feel like they came first, always.

"What do you guys think of staying in a lakeside cabin?" she asked.

Lars looked at her, his soft, brown eyes wide. Kyle didn't glance up from his math book. "Why would we stay in a cabin?" he asked.

"Just to get away from the house," she said.

That got Kyle to raise his head. "And why would we need to get away from the house?"

Cassie gave up trying to be nonchalant. "It could be an option if we needed to get away quickly and have someplace safe to hide. I have a friend—" She almost choked on the word. "Who owns a bunch of cabins on the lake. He says they're secluded and secure."

"Is that who asked you out?" Kyle asked.

Cassie decided to go with the truth. Her half-brothers deserved it. "Yes," she said. "But we're not going out."

"You should go out with him," Lars said. "You never date."

She blinked at them. "I don't have time to date."

"Sure, you do," Lars said. "Like right now, you could be on a date."

"Then who would be home with you? Making sure you get that history essay done?" She raised her eyebrows while he shrugged at her.

"It's not due until next week."

"Get the Chromebook, and let's get it done."

Lars groaned loudly, overemphasizing his displeasure, but he got up from the counter and went to get his computer.

"You really could go out with someone," Kyle said. "Mrs. Kim is real close, and like we decided this morning. We have time before anything drastic needs to happen."

"*If* anything drastic needs to happen," Cassie clarified.

"Right," Kyle said. "So you might as well go out with the guy. I mean, if you want to."

Oh, Cassie wanted to.

I'm really good at keeping secrets.

She was too, wasn't she? Wasn't that the foundation of the life she'd built here in Forbidden Lake?

Lars returned, and she let her thoughts of Jon meander wherever they would while she pointed out typos and grammar mistakes.

THE NEXT MORNING, ADDY POUNCED ON HER THE MOMENT she walked through the door. "So, are you going out with Dreamboat Addler?"

Cassie scoffed and laughed as she unwound the scarf from her neck. "No. Not even close." So she'd endured another sleepless night while she considered her options. That wasn't even entirely true, as it was two-twenty-five in the morning, and the night still had hours to go.

"Why not?" Addy asked, elbow-deep in dough already. "He is easily the hottest man to walk through that door in a week."

"That's only because Carlson didn't come in this week." She met her friend's eyes.

"Hey, I gave you forty-eight hours before I started with the questions."

"Addy, you've been crushing on that guy for months now. I've given you way more than forty-eight hours."

Addy said nothing. Just continued to knead the dough—or maybe her increased pounding of the innocent ingredients was her way of saying something.

They worked in the kitchen, the radio warbling out tunes from decades ago as the scent of yeast, sugar, and hot oil filled the air. Finally, Addy said, "So are you saying you have a crush on the handsome—scratch that. *Hot*—Jonathan Addler?"

Jon was handsome and hot. He was honest and hardworking. He was easy-going and teachable. He learned quickly, and he'd been fun to watch in the kitchen and delightful to flirt with.

So she had a massive crush on the guy. Didn't mean she was willing to risk her job to be with him. Did it?

"No," she said. "The university forbids relationships between professors and students, and he's in one of my classes."

"But you're both adults."

"So were the two who caused that big scandal last summer."

"Yeah, but there was a huge age difference. And she said he threatened her grade if she didn't sleep with him. You're not going to do that."

"It doesn't matter," Cassie said. "I'm not going to go out with him. I'm up for the full-time professorship job, and even His Hotness isn't worth risking that."

Addy giggled with Cassie at the title she'd given Jon. Then she said, "You might be wrong about that, Cassie. I think Jon is worth risking almost anything."

Her words went with Cassie through the rest of her shift and into her culinary courses for the day. She finished early on Fridays and was able to be home before the twins got off the bus. She had cookies in the oven and dinner halfway made when they walked in.

They acted as if nothing had changed, but Cassie felt like her whole life had been turned upside down the moment Jon had walked into her kitchen. She couldn't stop thinking about him, and she finally decided to text him as soon as she slid the homemade sausage and pepper Alfredo pizza into the oven.

But she didn't.

She put it off through dinner. Through a movie. Through

when the twins started playing video games after she'd told them they could stay up late because it was a weekend.

"I'm going to bed, guys," she finally said around eight o'clock. She didn't teach on the weekends, but she still went into the bakery in the middle of the night.

"'Night," they said together, which sent a rush of love through her for those good kids. She opened the door leading to the garage to make sure she'd closed the door after she'd come home, and she checked the front door to ensure it was locked.

Someone knocked while she still stood a foot from it, sending her pulse into palpitations. Button barked and barked, the high-pitched yapping doing nothing to calm Cassie's frenzied nerves.

Kyle and Lars came out of the living room, wearing identical expressions of worry.

She motioned for them to stay back, and she leaned forward to peer through the peephole that would allow her to see who stood on the porch.

It was Jonathan Addler.

CHAPTER SIX

J on knew someone was home; he'd been able to hear
the TV when he'd walked up the steps, and then it had
gone quiet. A small dog of some sort continued to
bark behind the still-closed door, and he wondered if
he should just go.

Text Cassie and arrange a meeting somewhere. But she'd
said nothing since the beginning of class yesterday, and he
wasn't sure he could wait until Tuesday night to see her again.

Scratch that. He absolutely could not wait until Tuesday
night to see her again. She consumed him, and he had to have
her in his life.

The dog stopped barking, and Jon faced the door, sure
someone was watching him through the peephole. The door
opened a few inches, and the porch light fell onto Cassie's
pretty face.

"Hey," he said. "Sorry to just drop by. I was—"

"Sh," she hissed. "Come inside." She stepped back, but the
door didn't open nearly wide enough to let his boxy shoulders
enter. He somehow squeezed through the narrow opening,

taking in the savory scent of sausage and cheese that lingered in the air.

Two teenagers stood in a nearby doorway, one of them holding a tiny dog that couldn't weigh more than ten pounds. His first inclination was to introduce himself to them, but he looked at Cassie first.

She wiped her palms down her thighs and looked at the boys too. "Jon, these are my brothers. Kyle and Lars. Guys, this is that friend I was telling you about. The one with the cabin."

Friend.

Jon liked the sound of that as much as he loathed it. The word definitely needed the addition of *boy* at the beginning.

"Hey," he said, lifting one hand in a wave. "What kind of dog is that?"

"He's a yorkie," one of the boys said. Jon would never be able to tell them apart, as they seemed identical right down to the way they stood.

"His name's Button," the other twin said.

"I have a dog," Jon said. "He's huge though."

"I didn't know you had a dog," Cassie said.

He gazed at her. "Well, there's a lot you don't know about me." His hunger for her obviously outweighed his humiliation at flirting with her right in front of her brothers.

"Yes," she said. "Like what you're doing here in the middle of the night."

"It's barely eight," he said.

"And I go to work in six and a half hours."

"Then let's talk quickly." He shot a glance at the boys, who'd clearly not lost interest in this conversation. "I believe you said you wanted another meeting to discuss terms."

He barely had time to look at Cassie before she grabbed onto his arm and hauled him away from the front door, the boys, the dog, and into the kitchen. He shouldn't be so excited by her anger, but he couldn't deny the zing of desire racing through him.

"How did you find me?" she asked, practically throwing his arm away from her once they were alone.

"Find you?" he repeated, straightening his sleeve. "Are you in hiding?"

Her jaw tightened, and several things came into focus for Jon. The nervousness in those boys' eyes. Her own anger—it wasn't anger at all, but pure fear.

"Cassie, are you in trouble?" he asked slowly, hoping the question wouldn't push her away.

"Of course not," she said, but he heard the note of falseness in her voice. "I just don't like strangers knocking on my door at night."

"I'm hardly a stranger."

Some of the fight and fire in her went out, leaving her shoulders slumped and her eyes weary. "I'm just tired. I was headed to bed when you knocked."

She looked tired, and the soft, gentle weariness in her eyes only endeared her more to him. "We can make it quick," he said, though nothing he did with Cassie should be done quickly. "You said you looked at the designs?"

"They were beautiful," she said, and he wondered if he really had caught her at her lowest. She'd never complimented him before, not even in class yesterday when his chicken was perfect. "I don't know what I want, but I'm sure I can have you build something."

"So our deal is on?"

She sighed and opened the fridge. The harsher light fell across her face, showing him the unrest in her expression. "I talked to my boss about hiring you to be my aide in class," she said. "She said we don't have the budget."

"So I'll remain a student," he said, thinking he'd like to be her anything-she-wanted.

She closed the fridge and looked anywhere but at him. "I can't date you if you're a student."

"And you could if we were co-workers?"

"No," she said slowly. "But at least it wouldn't carry so much risk."

"Cassie." He slid his fingers down her arm and into hers. He didn't know what else to say. He felt like he'd already put everything on the line, and she just needed to give him the green light.

"I haven't dated anyone in a long time," she whispered. "Not since getting guardianship of the boys. I promised our mom I'd take care of them." The pure vulnerability in her voice made Jon's heart weep for her.

"And I'm up for a full-time position at the university," she said. "Dating you puts all of that in jeopardy." She blinked, her eyes catching on his in the next moment. He saw honesty there. A little bit of fear, but that was at least overshadowed by the heat coursing between them.

"So we won't date," he said as casually as if he was mentioning that he liked cream in his coffee. "We can meet to discuss your project. And if I happen to hold your hand while we do that, well, it was an accident, right?"

Cassie smiled, a slow, sensual smile that sweetened as her eyes drifted closed. She leaned into him and rested her forehead against his chest. A simple motion. Something easy and light. And yet Jon felt like she had just given him permission to...well, he wasn't sure what. But she wasn't pushing him away.

"I shouldn't like you," she whispered. "It's not right."

"No?" He kept his voice as quiet as hers. "Well, then, it'll be our little secret." He pressed his lips to the top of her head, getting the scent of flowers and doughnuts in the same breath. "And just so you know, I haven't dated anyone in a while either." He couldn't believe he was going to start something real with her.

The image of Marcy's face danced through his mind. He'd been so hung up on her, and now he wasn't even sure why.

"Come on, you need to get to bed," he said.

"I'll walk you out." Cassie stepped out of his personal space but left her hand in his. They walked down the hall to the front door, where she gazed up at him like she wanted to kiss him good-night.

"Why don't you just drop the class?" she asked.

"I need it to finish my degree," he said, swallowing back his insane fantasies. "I'll tell you all about it another time." Or he wouldn't. He didn't particularly like delving into all the reasons he felt inadequate, one of which was that the rest of his brothers had managed to finish college and earn their father's respect. Jon hadn't.

Yet, he told himself.

He only had a few classes left, a couple of them easy electives like this culinary arts one. So he'd been planning to kill two birds with one stone—get Marcy to go out with him and check off another box toward his diploma.

He put two fingers under her chin and gently lifted her face so she was looking at him. "You can trust me, you know," he said. "I know there's something bothering you."

"How did you find my house?" she asked, more curiosity in her voice now than accusation.

Discomfort squirreled through Jon. "I have a business management class on Friday afternoons. I may have looked up your schedule and waited for you to finish. Then I just followed you." He couldn't believe he'd admitted to stalking. Out loud. Embarrassment clawed at his stomach, especially when the softness in her eyes turned to glass.

"I've been home for hours," she said.

"Yeah, I ran home to take my dog out, and then I sort of just drove around a little bit."

Cassie searched his face, and he had no idea if she found what she was looking for or not. "So anyone could follow me home."

Confusion hit him in the chest. "I guess so." He cocked his head, trying to read her expression. "Cassie, I know you're hiding something from me."

"It's time for you to go," she said, stepping out of his reach completely and wrapping her fingers around the doorknob.

"Cassie."

"We barely know each other, Jon. Of course I'm hiding things from you." She didn't open the door yet, and he remembered how he'd slipped inside through a tiny opening.

"Maybe I could help you."

"Maybe." She nodded toward the door. "Are you ready to go?"

"No." He put his hand over hers on the knob, the flame in his gut roaring back to life with the contact. "And if we keep getting to know each other, will you tell me what you're hiding from me?"

"Maybe."

He smiled at her, mostly to conceal his frustration. "You know, I liked that word when you texted it to me the other day. Now? Not so much."

"Good-night, Jon." She opened the door, the conversation clearly over.

He hesitated, and lasers practically shot from her eyes. So he exited her house, unsurprised to hear the door click before he'd even settled both feet on the front porch and the lock slide into place.

Oh, yes. Cassie Caldwell was definitely hiding something.

Or hiding from someone. He hadn't made it to the warmth of his car when his phone chimed.

And I'd love to talk to you about renting a cabin too, she said. *What do you think about that?*

No *thanks for coming.* No *it was great to see you.* No *I wish you would've kissed me.*

Jon smiled and chuckled as he got behind the wheel and started his car. He couldn't be outside in the cold while he texted. But with the heater blowing, he managed to answer her with, *Maybe.*

CHAPTER SEVEN

Cassie couldn't sleep after Jon left. And she'd been looking forward to finally getting some rest. But she tossed and turned, pulled at the too-tight blanket, and wished she had Button with her. But the twins had taken the yorkie into their bedroom that night. At least they were sleeping in their own room again.

Even holding hands with Jon was wrong. She shouldn't have done it. Shouldn't have told him anything about her past dating life, her brothers, or the professorship. And yet, at the same time, something had released in her chest when she'd shared personal things with him.

She picked up her phone and looked at that stupid *Maybe* he'd sent. An idea strobed in her mind, and she seized onto it. Instead of thinking it through and making a list of pros and cons, she acted on it.

I have to leave early in the morning, she sent to Addy. *Four or so. Hope that's okay.*

She knew her best friend wouldn't answer, as Addy was diligent in her sleep schedule and went to bed by seven PM every night.

And with a plan in mind, Cassie was finally able to drift to sleep.

By four o'clock in the morning, she'd rushed through the doughnut prep and explained everything to Addy. So when her friend said, "Go get him, Cass," Cassie was able to leave the bakery with confidence in her step and determination in her mind.

Mile by mile and minute by minute, she lost the feelings she'd had at the bakery. By the time she peered up at the sign proclaiming that she'd arrived at Sunshine Shores Cherry Orchard and Resort, she wanted to turn around and head back to town.

She felt like she'd gone completely crazy. But Jon had come to the shop, and she needed to see him when there was no one else around. He'd said he had a cabin on the family plot of land, but she didn't know anything about where that would be.

She pulled out her phone and called him, some of her bravery returning. "There's no way he's awake," she muttered to herself.

"Hey," he said, without any grogginess in his voice.

"Oh, you are awake."

"Unfortunately. Goliath had to take care of business."

"So are you outside?"

"Standing on my porch."

"Which road do I turn down to find that?"

Silence came through the line, and then he sputtered with a chuckle. "You're here?"

"You came to my shop to talk."

"Oh, so we're going to talk."

A multitude of other things paraded through her head, but Cassie said, "Yes, I need to talk to you."

"I suppose that's acceptable. Where are you?"

She explained what roads she'd gone down, and where she was currently parked.

"So we're down the road to the south. Get back on the one you drove down, and keep going past the one you came in on from town. There's another one a bit down. Turn left, and come on down. You'll see me. Fourth cabin in."

"A cabin?" Cassie put her car in reverse and pulled out of the spot she'd stopped in.

"I mean, it's made of wood."

"This place is impressive. Must do well."

"Yes," he said.

"So you're rich," she said, not really asking.

"Yes," he said.

"And you still run your own carpentry firm?" She went past the road that led back to town.

"Yes."

"Are you only going to say yes this morning?" She turned and caught sight of him standing on the porch down the road, just as he said he'd be. He wore a pair of joggers and a thick, black coat, which made him absolutely...normal. Human.

"Depends on the question," he said.

"So that's a no." She pulled into his driveway, noticing that yes, this house was made of wood, but it was so much more than a cabin. Even the front door looked like it cost more than her car.

She killed the engine and got out of the car, the bitter cold biting against her exposed skin. Ending the call, she walked toward him, glancing left and right. When she looked back at him, she caught him doing the same thing.

"Let me open the garage," he said. "You can pull in there."

"Good idea." She returned to the car and pulled into the garage, parking beside his truck and getting out as he closed the door behind her, concealing her and her car.

He *was* very good at keeping secrets.

Jon stood in the doorway leading into the house, and he didn't budge as she came up the few steps to join him. "You didn't like my maybe," he said.

"I didn't."

He swept one arm around her and pulled her close to his body. He leaned down and touched his lips to her forehead, sending heat and tingles through her whole body. A dog barked from somewhere, and Jon moved away from her. "Let me get Goliath."

"He sounds scary," she said, following him into the warm house.

"He's just big," Jon said. "But he's gentle." He crossed through the kitchen to the back door and opened it to let in a huge brown dog with black facial features. "He's a mastiff. Go say hello, bud."

Goliath came over to Cassie, and he did seem happy to see her. He was enormous, and he put his wet, snowy front paws on her shoulders, nearly knocking her down.

"Down," Jon said, and the dog obeyed instantly. For some reason, Cassie liked that, and she glanced at Jon.

"I wanted to rent a cabin," she said.

"Great," he said. "You can call our front office for that. They open at nine in the winter." He leaned against the counter, and with his movie star hair all rumpled from bed, Cassie could only think of him there.

She glanced toward the hallway to her left, wondering if he had a king-size bed or not. Someone like him probably did.

She looked back at him and caught him yawning. "Sorry to keep you from going back to bed. I'll go."

He darted forward and latched onto her wrist. "Don't go." He dipped his head again, pressing his mouth against her temple, then her cheek, his nose tracing a path lower and lower until he finally kissed her neck.

A growl ground through his throat, and he whispered, "You better start talking if that's what you really want to do."

Instead of saying anything in words, Cassie arched into his touch, fire burning through her whole body as he ran his hands up her back and down to her waist again. He definitely had good hands. Such good hands.

"I have to tell you something," she said, her voice made more of air than anything.

"Mm," he said, sliding his mouth to her ear.

She managed to press her palms against his chest and apply pressure. He backed up, and when he opened his eyes and looked at her, there was a definite heated haze in his expression.

She felt buzzed herself, like she'd been drinking, something she never did, especially now that she had the twins. She couldn't afford to let her guard down, to not be aware of everything and everyone around her.

And yet, Jon made her forget all of her precautions.

"I'm not really in hiding," she started. "But you freaked me out, showing up at my house last night."

Jon retreated back to the counter, where he started making coffee. "Why's that?"

"Because the twins' father just got out of prison on parole, and we're all worried he's going to come for them."

Jon glanced up at her, those hands stilling in the coffee prep. "He's dangerous?"

"Abusive," she said. "My mom was only with him for a few years before she divorced him. But before she died, she told me all she'd done to keep them safe from Larry. I promised her I'd continue what she'd done."

He went back to making coffee, his eyebrows drawn down now. She found him just as sexy with the thoughtful frown on his face, and she walked over to the counter and took a seat on the barstool.

"So I'm a little nervous when people knock on my door at night." She glanced around the high-end kitchen, with its black stainless appliances, complete with a fridge that had a screen on it that listed the contents.

"What kind of fridge is that?" she asked.

"Oh, this is a one-of-a-kind," he said, turning to it. "Charles, tell me if I have cream for my coffee."

"You have two quarts of cream," a robotic voice said. "One is hazelnut flavored. The other plain vanilla."

Cassie blinked at the fridge. "That's ridiculous."

"Yeah, and it never got off the ground anyway." He opened the fridge and pulled out the two quarts of coffee creamer. Nodding behind her, he said, "That one will tell you a joke."

Cassie turned and saw the two-foot-tall robot on the counter. She looked back at Jon. "I thought you were into woodworking. Good with your hands and all that."

"Oh, I am," he said with a flirty smile. "But I also have a little obsession with StartUp.com. Anything techy or cool, and I throw a few bucks at it."

"So that's how you got the fridge that keeps track of what's inside it."

"That's right."

She walked over to the robot, and his eyes opened before she said anything. "Oh, hello. Do you want to know the weather today?"

A giggle escaped from her mouth before she could suck it back in. "No," she said. "Tell me a joke instead."

"How do you make a handkerchief dance? You put a little boogie in it."

Cassie burst into laughter, leaning into Jon as he joined her and slipped his arm around her. His laughter joined with hers, and Cassie's secret crush on this gorgeous man doubled.

And he was her gorgeous *student*, and that made her laughter dry up into silence.

"So," she said. "I'd like to rent a cabin, just so we have it if we need...somewhere else to go sometimes."

"Oh, you're talking a permanent rental?" he asked.

"Do you do things like that?"

"I honestly don't know," he said. "But I can find out. I know we have a couple of other properties that aren't being used right now, too. I can ask my brother about those."

"Your brother?"

"Yeah, Liam runs the rentals, and he manages all our land."

"Oh, he sounds like a barrel of fun."

"He is, actually. Has a little girl named Kimmie. She's the cutest thing on the planet." He reached up to open a cabinet and pulled down two mugs. "I know you like coffee. Cream and sugar?"

"Yes," she said, following him back into the kitchen. He poured her coffee and mixed in what she liked, and there was nothing sexier than him making coffee for her. Oh, wait. Maybe there was—the tender way he spoke about his niece.

"Is your brother married, then?" she asked.

"He was," Jon said. "His wife died a few years ago. My oldest sister, Karly, she's married. And my youngest, Mia, has a boyfriend. The rest of us are kind of in between relationships right now." He lifted his coffee cup to his lips and sipped, and Cassie couldn't help tracking the movement.

A sense of safety enveloped her, and Cassie didn't know what to make of that. But it felt normal to be standing in his kitchen with him, drinking coffee, and talking about his family.

"Are you really in between relationships?" she asked.

He flinched, which caused his creamed up coffee to spill onto the back of his hand. He swore under his breath and turned toward the sink, which he flipped onto to cold and put his hand underneath the flow of water.

When he turned back to her, he gazed evenly at her. "I suppose not," he said. "What about you?"

Cassie shrugged and sipped her coffee. "We'd have to be really good at keeping this secret." She couldn't believe she'd said it. Couldn't believe she was even considering perpetuating this relationship. Couldn't get the feel of his lips on her face and neck out of her mind.

"Then you should probably go," he said. "Before the rest of my family wakes up and sees you driving out of here like we spent the night together." He picked up his coffee mug and drank from it again, his dark, dangerous eyes gleaming at her.

Cassie tried not to scamper out of his house, obeying exactly what he said, but she did precisely that. And as the secret of her and Jon burrowed deep into her heart, she felt warm from head to toe.

CHAPTER EIGHT

"**Y**ou better be careful, Jon," Karly said as she lifted the lid on one of the pizza boxes.

"I'm always careful," Jon said. Karly had indeed seen Cassie "slinking away" from Jon's house at five-thirty in the morning, and she'd shown up only minutes later.

A week had passed since then, and Jon had only seen Cassie in class on Tuesday and Thursday evenings. They'd texted a lot, and he'd found out that there were two family cabins that Cassie could use any time she wanted.

"Free," Liam had said. "If you need it, Jon, you can have it." He'd been distracted by Kimmie's upset stomach, and Jon felt like he'd gotten away with something by not having to explain to his brother exactly what he needed the cabin for.

But Karly had asked at least a thousand questions, and Jon had answered them all. So she knew Cassie was a professor at the college, and that Jon had fallen hard for her.

"I didn't mean with her," Karly said, hooking him with her big-sister eyes.

"I'm fine," Jon said.

"You abandoned Marcy in less than an hour," Karly said, her head moving a little too much like a bobble-head doll.

"First off," Jon said, getting up to snag a piece of pizza before everyone else arrived. "There was nothing between Marcy and me. Nothing to abandon."

"But you liked her for so long."

"And now I like Cassie," Jon said. He couldn't explain the shift that had happened in the kitchen, only that it had. And he'd felt it, almost like God himself moving the earth so that Jon would be forced to see the woman standing in front of him. "Don't worry, Curls. We haven't even kissed yet."

Karly scowled at his childhood nickname for her and shook her head. "I don't believe you."

"Believe what you want. She didn't stay the night last weekend." No matter how much Jon wished that were true. "And don't say anything to Phoenix either. I heard from Sami that the Department is causing him grief again."

"It's not the DNR," Karly said. "But a certain blonde who works for them."

Jon chuckled at the very thought of Phoenix with a woman. Not because his brother didn't deserve to share his remote cabin with someone that loved him. But because Phoenix himself was so cut off to the outside world—and the opportunity to find someone again—that it would never happen.

Of course, Jon had never been engaged before—never even been in love—so he couldn't fault Phoenix for his anti-female stance after his fiancée had left him standing at the altar.

"And don't say anything else," Jon said as the front door to their parents' house opened. "Okay, Karly? You sometimes slip up when there's so many people to entertain."

"I do not," she said. "I'm as good at secrets as you are." She flipped her dark hair over her shoulder and turned to greet Mia and her boyfriend. Jon watched his sisters talk and interact, feeling a bit removed from them tonight.

The family always got together on Sunday evenings for dinner at the big house on the edge of the orchard where they'd all grown up. Jon normally loved the vibrancy that came from five siblings, grandparents, his niece, and anyone else who came.

But tonight, he just wanted to spend a quiet evening with Cassie and her brothers. He'd texted her, but she hadn't responded yet—which meant she wasn't going to. He wasn't invited.

They'd both made bold moves over the past couple of weeks, but Jon didn't want to explain his absence to his family, and he didn't want to leave Karly here alone without him here to make sure she didn't spill his secret relationship to the rest of the family.

One by one, they all arrived, and Jon put on his party face. After all, he didn't need his sisters zeroing in on him and asking him about Marcy. Or anything else.

He avoided his father too, but his dad still managed to sidle up next to him and ask, "How are the classes going, Jon?"

"Just great," he said. "I made the salad tonight, in fact."

"You're taking cooking?"

"I needed one more elective," he said. "It was that or bowling or something equally as stupid." He picked up his can of soda and drained the last of it. "I have business management homework, so I think I'm going to take off early."

"And how many classes do you have until you graduate?"

Jon bristled at the question, mostly because his dad knew the answer already. They'd had this conversation so many times. But he simply gazed into his father's dark eyes, so much like his own, and said, "Just two, Dad. The business math class and the finance class for small businesses." His dad couldn't sue him for putting the math classes off until last. The subject had never been Jon's strong suit. Sure, he could measure and get pieces of wood to line up to the sixteenth-inch. But he didn't need to balance accounts or complete calculus problems to make a dresser.

"So next Christmas, you'll be done."

"If I don't go in the summer," Jon said coolly.

"Well, you can't go in the summer," his dad said. "It's our busiest time of the year."

Your busiest time of the year, Jon wanted to say. But he just smiled a tight, closed-mouth smile at his father and edged over to his mom. "I'm headed out early," he said, sweeping a kiss along her cheek. "Love you, Mom."

"Oh, Jon, wait. Something came to the house for Phoenix. He didn't take it before he left. You'll see him soon, won't you?" She bustled away before Jon could confirm that yes, he'd see Phoenix soon. Why his brother had only stayed for twenty minutes would also be discussed, and Jon wanted first-hand information about the blonde with the Department of Natural Resources.

So he took the large envelope from his mother and sauntered out of the house like he'd rather stay than go do homework. But he wasn't going to do his homework right now anyway—unless copious amounts of texting with his secret girlfriend counted. If it did, then he totally was going to do homework.

JON ARRIVED A HALF-HOUR EARLY TO TUESDAY'S CLASS, hoping to find Cassie alone for just a few minutes. But two other students had already arrived, turning his romantic surprise into a complete flop. After all, he couldn't give her a red rose and a bag of Skittles—her favorite fruity candy—when he was supposed to be nothing more than a student.

She'd said nothing else about the cabin or having him make something for her, so he sat in the back of the class and detailed that he had presents for her in his car, and if she wanted, they could meet after class so she could get them.

Then he told her he'd picked up the key to the cabin she could use whenever she wanted to, and that she should probably come to his house in the morning to get it. *Really early*, he said. *Like last time.*

He saw her head move as she checked her phone each time he texted. A smile rode her mouth too, but she didn't pick up her device to respond.

And you should probably hire me to build something for you, he sent last. *That way, we can show that we knew each other before this class started. I don't want you to lose your job.*

And he didn't want to lose his credits at Northwestern Michigan College. He'd been working on his degree for years, and he didn't know if they could take his credits from him or not. But he had assumed some risk in their forbidden relationship too.

She finally picked up her phone, her fingers flying over the screen as her dark hair fell in a veil between them. He wanted to run his fingers through it desperately, and if he didn't kiss her soon, he felt sure he'd combust. His heart, his lungs, all of him.

I'm deleting all of these texts, she sent. *You should too. I'll see you in the morning.*

Jon couldn't help grinning like a fool as he deleted the text string between him and Cassie. He'd named her Goliath in his phone, and he'd been careful to delete their messages every single night. She did too.

The thrill of having something secret swept through Jon as she got up and entered the kitchen. Surprise lit her face when she saw him there already, but he pretended to look at something else.

After all, he'd told her he was very good at keeping secrets, and he really wanted to be. His whole relationship with her depended on it.

THE FOLLOWING MORNING, HE WAITED ON THE FRONT porch of the cabin Liam had said Cassie could use whenever she needed to. He'd texted her the directions, and he'd left his big mastiff at home.

The woods surrounding the cabin were quiet, muted by the newly fallen snow. The white stuff continued to fall, making everything serene and simple beyond the porch, and Jon rediscovered why he loved Michigan so much.

Cassie's tires made squishing noises as she pulled up to the cabin, and she used his footprints, hopping and jumping from one to the other until she reached the bottom stair. Then she approached slower, her hands tucked deep in her coat pockets.

"The purple looks good on you," he said, rising to greet her. Could he kiss her right here, right now? Did she have anything else to tell him? "And hey, I tried the steak and eggs again this morning, and there were no flames."

She trilled out a laugh that sounded so loud out here in the wilderness. "Those flames were Colton's."

"I know, but I thought you'd like to know that I got the dish right."

She put both hands behind his neck and swayed with him like they were at a high school prom. "I have no doubt. You're very good with your hands."

"Oh, you're a little flirty this morning, aren't you?" He grinned at her and dropped his gaze to her mouth.

"Not more than you. You think I believe you've been up since four, making steak and eggs?"

"Are you calling me a liar?"

"If the boot fits." She shrugged, her smile so filled with coy wattage, he was almost blinded by it.

"Come on, then," he said, dropping his hands from her waist and turning to enter the cottage. "So Liam says we own this one for family use, but no one's using it right now. He said I could access it whenever I wanted." He opened the door, glad Cassie had come with him and slipped her hand into his.

"It's pretty empty, but there are some basics. I was thinking I'd bring out some staples as far as food goes, so if you do have to retreat here, you'll have the essentials." He looked around at the single couch in the living room. The kitchen sat at the back of the house, and besides the groceries he'd brought in last night to make her breakfast, he knew the cupboards and fridge were empty.

"Thank you, Jon," she said in a voice he rarely heard—one filled with emotion and gratitude.

He glanced at her, making a decision on the spot. He used those hands she claimed were so great, and took her face in both of them. "I hope you never have to use it," he whispered just before lowering his head to kiss her.

This time, he didn't seek her permission by lighting kisses on her forehead and then her cheeks, hoping she'd give him the go-ahead to kiss her properly.

He just did it, fireworks popping through his mouth and down his throat at the way her mouth fit exactly against his. Her fingernails tracked along his scalp, causing a moan to emanate from deep within his stomach, and Jon enjoyed this kiss with her more than he'd enjoyed anything else in his entire life.

CHAPTER NINE

Cassie had been kissed before, but never like this. Jon's mouth was both demanding and firm against hers, yet gentle and probing too. He hadn't asked, and yet it felt like he needed permission to deepen the kiss.

So she did it, opening her mouth a bit wider so he'd know she was okay with this kiss. And wow, what a kiss.

He moved his mouth to her neck again, and she sucked at the air as she held onto his powerful shoulders. "Jon," she whispered, but he claimed her mouth again before she could say anything else.

She'd never felt this much energy pouring through her before, and she wondered if that was what love felt like. She'd never been in love before, not with a man she wanted to kiss and kiss and kiss until they fell asleep together, exhausted from the emotions streaming between them.

He finally pulled away and rested his forehead against her shoulder. She held him close to her, bent over as he was, and felt like she'd finally found someone she could share her life with. She hadn't even realized she wanted someone like him.

"I looked you up," she finally said, her confession for the day.

"Oh?" He straightened and looked into her eyes, those magical hands kneading their way up her back and down to her waist again.

"Yeah, you only have two more classes until you graduate with your business management degree."

"Oh," he said again.

"You didn't tell me you were actually earning a degree from the university."

"Didn't I?"

"Jon," she said as he disentangled himself from her arms and moved into the kitchen. "You know you didn't."

"I guess I didn't think it important."

"I thought you were just taking my class for another woman."

"What's the difference?" He pulled a pan out of the oven. "And I did get here early to make steak and eggs, I'll have you know."

The food distracted her for a few moments, the over-easy eggs cooked to perfection. "Wow, Jon. You're like, perfect."

He laughed. "I'm sure my father would love to tell you all of my flaws." He set a small salt and pepper shaker set on the counter. "Let's eat. Getting up early really works up the appetite, doesn't it?" He picked up a fork and slid one to her before coming around to the other side of the bar and sitting beside her.

She ate for a few minutes, the tang of the eggs with the perfectly cooked steak amazing. "You aren't worried you'll lose your degree if we're caught?"

"We're not going to get caught," he said. "I honestly don't see why it matters. The only reason that other professor got in trouble was because he threatened the girl's grade." He cut her a look. "She went to the administration. I'm not going to do that."

Cassie nodded, but she felt like her head had been partially severed from her neck. "What if things between us don't work out?" she asked.

"Then they don't work out," he said. "I've had women break up with me before."

"So you won't be breaking up with me?" She thought of the kiss they'd just shared, and she'd felt Jon's emotion for her. It was as strong as her own and burned just as brightly.

"Not today," he said evasively, and Cassie let the conversation drop. She didn't need his reassurance that he liked her. He'd just kissed her like she'd never been kissed before, and that had said everything.

"I brought a back-dated contract," he said. "You should sign it before you go."

"Am I sneaking out only minutes after arriving again today?"

"Not necessarily," he said. "It's up to you. My, uh, sister may have seen you leave last time."

"What?" she asked, sudden fear gripping her heart with a cold, iron fist.

"But did you see the gate you came through to get to this place?" He indicated a set of two keys on the counter beside her. "The gold one goes to the padlock on that gate. No one can get in or out without it."

She nodded, the extra layer of security comforting. "Which sister?"

"Karly, the oldest."

"And?" she prompted when he didn't continue.

"And nothing. She's married. She gets it."

Cassie frowned and finished eating. "Gets what, Jon?"

He looked at her, those dark eyes drawing her further and further into whatever existed between them. "Honestly?"

"I think honesty would be best," she said. "I don't want to have to keep too many lies straight."

"You're lying? To who? Your bakery boss?"

"Not really, I guess. Addy knows I'm leaving early to come see you." She sounded a bit defeated, even to her own ears. "So I guess we're both failing at keeping this a secret." Maybe she should break up with him right now. Tell him he was a bad kisser and never speak to him again. But then, that would be a lie she'd have to keep straight.

"I think we're doing fine," he said, reaching for her hand.

"So what were you going to say?" she asked. "About your sister getting something?"

"I don't know." He exhaled. "I guess she just gets my insane desire to be with you."

"You think that it's insane to want to be with me?" She may have screeched the last couple of words.

Jon only chuckled and took her fully into his arms again. "I know I feel like I'm going mad when I'm not with you," he whispered just before he kissed her again.

CASSIE FLOATED THROUGH THE NEXT MONTH, WAKING WITH a smile on her face despite the early hour and humming through her morning job. Addy had stopped asking questions about Jon, and Cassie left the bakery every morning at five when they opened.

Anyone watching would think she just had a new routine. Of course, anyone watching would see she went out to Sunshine Shores every morning too. But she never went to Jon's again, instead taking a bag of groceries or a suitcase with extra clothes to the cabin in the middle of nowhere.

Over the course of the weeks, she managed to fill it with everything she, Kyle, or Lars would need should they ever have to use the cabin to hide in. By her estimation, she had three weeks' worth of food and supplies for the three of them, and enough fuel to keep them warm and the stove going.

The smoke concerned her, but as the days passed and she received absolutely no word about Larry, some of her fears faded. She'd done daily searches on him as well, and the papers weren't reporting anything.

Each evening, she kept her brothers up-to-date with her findings—which were nothing at this point. It certainly made her morning meetings with her carpenter a lot more fun. Because she didn't have to worry so much about Larry, she could focus on her secret boyfriend.

They had a private date for Valentine's Day that evening. She'd asked her neighbor to keep an eye on the twins, who she'd told she was going out with someone completely different than "the man who'd shown up one night" at their house. She certainly didn't want the twins to know she was dating one of her students, and if she and Jon got caught....

She pushed the thought from her mind as she set her coffee on her desk and opened her laptop. The office off the kitchen was cold, as usual, and she reached down to the space heater under her desk and switched it on.

After tapping a few times and yawning more than that, she navigated to her email account. She had regular office hours, but her students typically emailed her if they were having a problem, needed to miss class, or whatever.

She had a few messages from students she fielded quickly, and then her eyes landed on one from Dr. Langstrom. *Available for an interview on Friday?*

Her heartbeat started ricocheting around inside her chest. Friday. That was three days from now, if today didn't count. Her fingers shook as she opened the email to see that if she wanted to interview for the full-time professorship position in the Family and Consumer Science department, Food Services division, she'd need to be ready on Friday morning at eight-fifteen.

"Eight-fifteen," she whispered. That was barely enough time for breakfast with Jon and then to flit home, get showered, and get the twins off to school. If she had a teleporter, she could make it to the college by eight-fifteen, but otherwise....

Sure, she typed into the email. *I'll be there at eight-fifteen.*

And if she knew Dr. Langstrom—and she did—Cassie would need to be early. So she couldn't drive the boys to school that morning. They rode the bus home in the afternoon, but she liked dropping them off behind the locked gate, just to make sure they got there safely.

"They can text you," she muttered to herself. She added, *Thank you for the opportunity*, read through the few words again to make sure she hadn't made any typos, and sent the message back to Dr. Langstrom.

She exhaled as she leaned away from her desk. Super keyed-up now, she didn't need the caffeine in the cup in front of her, but she lifted it to her lips anyway.

A return email popped up, and it was sort of freaky to think that Dr. Langstrom was up in her office in the same building, reading and responding to her email. Cassie tapped to open it.

Great. Bring two letters of recommendation.

Cassie's heart dropped to her toes. Two letters of recommendation? She didn't have letters of recommendation, and she had no idea who to ask. She'd never taught in the higher education system until she'd relocated to Forbidden Lake, and her experience in professional kitchens had gotten her the associate professor job.

She had the letters she'd used back then, and perhaps she could use them again....

The idea got dismissed quickly. Dr. Langstrom had already seen those letters. No, Cassie needed new stuff she could use to get the job. She grabbed her phone and sent a text to Addy. It would be a similar letter, but at least it would be new.

After sending the text, asking her best friend to write a letter for her, Cassie stared straight ahead, wondering where else she could get a letter about her teaching specifically. Dr. Langstrom had done two evaluations of her, so the woman already knew how she taught.

Cassie wondered who else would be interviewed, who she was up against for the job.

Maybe she could ask a past student to testify about her stellar teaching in the kitchen.

Or a present student.

"Don't be stupid," she said to herself, glancing out the door to make sure no one from her noon class had shown up yet. She had a student coming to try last week's recipe that she'd bungled, and Cassie didn't need to be talking to herself when the student showed up.

But she was not going to ask Jon for a letter of recommendation.

"Hey, Miss Caldwell."

She looked at the blonde college student who had just arrived. "Hey, Molly."

"You said I could practice before class?" She hooked her thumb over her shoulder.

"Yeah." Cassie stood up. "Yep. There's all the ingredients in the fridge. Go for it."

Molly smiled, hitched her backpack higher on her shoulder, and turned.

"Molly?" Cassie stepped out of her office. "I'm up for a full-time professorship here, and I need a letter of recommendation. Do you think—have you ever done something like that?"

Molly blinked a couple of times. "I haven't."

"It's simple, really," she said. "You just tell them how amazing of a teacher I am." She smiled at the girl, who smiled back.

"I can do that."

"Thank you." Cassie indicated the refrigerator in the back of the room. "Go on then. Class starts soon."

CHAPTER TEN

Jon knew the moment Cassie arrived at the cabin. He noticed every little thing she brought into it too, from the empty suitcases to the clothes she'd put in the dressers in both bedrooms. Some were hers, and some obviously belonged to the twins. She'd brought extra pillows for the bed and more firewood than this cottage needed for an entire winter.

And the food. Wow, she'd brought in a lot of non-perishable food.

Jon realized how worried she was about the Larry Glassman she'd told him about as he watched more and more being brought into the house. She'd told him more about the man and how abusive and controlling he was. According to her, Larry Glassman stood over six feet tall and had biceps made of steel.

He didn't have a nice bone in his body, and he'd shot two people in a gas station one night while he was drunk. Neither of them died, so he'd been eligible for parole after twelve years in prison.

The articles Jon had read had labeled Larry as a terrible

person, but he'd gotten parole, because he followed all the rules and the judge found him worthy of re-entering society.

Jon didn't know anyone in Chicago to help feed him inside information, but Cassie said she still had loyal friends there, and they'd told her nothing.

The front door opened, and Jon turned from his thoughts the same way he turned from the vase of red roses on the kitchen counter. "Hey, beautiful," he said, smiling at her. He'd enjoyed this last month with her immensely, and he'd even gotten used to getting up at four-thirty in the morning.

Sure, it made his evenings exhausting, but the only person who'd noticed lived in another remote cabin on family land, and Phoenix had stopped asking Jon to dinner after the first couple of times Jon had declined.

"Happy Valentine's Day," she said, closing and locking the door behind her. She held a red-wrapped package in her hands, and she smiled at him in that half-sexy, half-flirty way she had that set his blood on fire.

"Mm, Happy Valentine's Day," he said, taking her into his arms and kissing her. Jon loved kissing her. Holding her close and breathing in the sweet scent of her hair. She claimed that came from all the sugar in the bakery, as he normally only saw her in the mornings after her shift in the shop.

But tonight, she smelled just as sugary, and he knew her last class had ended at three. He slid his hands over her shoulders and up into her hair, taking the ponytail holder out so her dark waves streamed through his fingers.

He loved her hair. Loved the way she laid in his arms while they cuddled on the couch after breakfast in the morning. Loved how she'd told him stories about her mother, her time at culinary school, her trials in raising the twins for the past fifteen months.

He loved learning what she liked to eat and what she didn't. He loved sharing his life with her, and as Jon kissed her on the most romantic day of the year, he wondered if he was simply in love with her.

The thought terrified and excited him at the same time, and he pulled away though Cassie was kissing him as hungrily as he was her.

"Okay," he said, stepping back and wiping his hands down the front of his jeans the way he did when he needed a minute to think about a project. "You said you were bringing dinner? I only brought dessert."

"Did you make it like you promised?"

"I sure did," he said, pride swelling within him. "But we're not eating dessert first." He watched her as she came closer. "Are we?"

She slid her hands up his chest. "I got an interview for the full-time professorship on Friday."

Happiness burst through him. "That's great."

She tipped up onto her toes and kissed him again, this time with a little more passion, a little more fervor, a little more heat. He went with it, because he liked their rougher kisses as well as the more gentle, tender way she kissed him.

She pulled away as quickly as she'd started, and her eyes locked onto his. "I really need this job."

"And you'll get it," he said.

She closed her eyes and nodded, and in that single moment, Jon felt sure he was in love with her. Karly would be so mad at him for not being careful, for not slowing himself down a little bit.

Cassie stepped out of his arms and said, "So I brought those sweet and sour meatballs you love. Mashed potatoes. And my students made sides today, so we have a lot of samples to choose from." She walked backward away from him, her eyes glittering with flirty fun he couldn't wait to have. "Come help me, Mister Muscles."

He chuckled. "Oh, so now I know what I'm good for."

She giggled too, turned around and continued toward the front door, that extra sway in her hips definitely just for him. After all, he'd seen her walk around the kitchen during class, and she didn't use the same motion.

He went outside with her, glad the worst of the winter seemed to be behind them. In another month, the cherry trees would be blossoming, and he couldn't wait to walk with Cassie, her hand in his, beneath the fragrant flowers.

She passed him a stack of aluminum trays, and he took them into the cottage. With the door once again closed and locked behind them, Cassie took the lid off the meatballs, letting out a puff of steam. "Mashed potatoes," she said. "And let's see what the students turned in." She removed the lid from the first tray and he saw green beans and bacon, creamed corn, and what looked like sweet potato hash.

"These all look good," he said, snagging a single square of sweet potato and popping it into his mouth. "Oh, that's spicy." He coughed. "Really spicy." He started around the counter to the sink for a drink while Cassie took a bite too.

"It's not that bad," she said as he downed a full glass of water. "And you should drink milk to cool the heat."

Jon coughed, his stomach already full from the water. But he poured himself some milk and drank that too, the chili powder finally fading against his palette.

"So your entertainment center is going great," he said. "I have some pictures from earlier today if you'd like to see them." He made sure he brought up the carpentry project she'd technically hired him to build every time they got together. Then, if he was ever questioned, he could say that of course they met, because she wanted information on the project she'd hired him about.

"Sure, let me see them."

So Jon got out his work device and logged in, creating another record of the business between them. "I put the shelves on today for the twins' game machine, as well as the Blu-ray player. See?" He turned the tablet toward her, and she studied the pictures.

"Beautiful work," she said, smiling at the pictures.

He tapped on the screen and then pinched to rotate it. "Ignore the messy shop."

"I still want to see the messy shop," she said, bumping him with her hip.

"Yeah, well, I'd like the twins to know about us, but sometimes we don't get what we want."

Cassie pulled in a breath, and Jon wished he could yank the words back into his mouth as easily.

"I mean—"

"We've talked about this," she said.

"No," Jon said slowly, not wanting to ruin Valentine's Day with this beautiful woman. "*We've* never talked about it. You *told* me I wasn't allowed to be your boyfriend in public."

"Jon."

"But the twins wouldn't tell anyone," he said. "Your house isn't really public, Cass."

"They might slip up," she said.

"And tell who? A friend at school who doesn't know me? Or you? I think you put too much stock in teenagers caring about what their parents do." Jon shook his head and got down two plates. "It doesn't matter. I'm starving, and I never see you at night, and I don't want to argue."

The resulting silence in the cottage berated Jon for saying anything, and when he handed a plate to Cassie, she simply glared at him. "You signed on to be a secret," she said. "I'm your little secret too. You think I don't want to parade you all over town?"

"I don't know, Cassie. I don't know what you want." He scooped up a spoonful of mashed potatoes.

"That's ridiculous," she said. "I've told you everything

about me. Everything I've been working for. Everything I dream about."

Jon's chest felt hollow, and he wasn't sure why. Cassie had told him all of that, and he wasn't sure why he'd said she didn't. "You're right," he said, his emotions still warring inside him. "I guess I just...what happens if you get the full-time professorship?"

"Then what I've been working for is achieved," she said. "A stable life for Kyle and Lars. No more early-morning bakery hours."

He glanced at her, wondering if she heard all she was saying. "So you'd stay in town permanently," he said slowly, focusing back on his plate of food. "So no need for this cottage in the woods, which you've filled with clothes, supplies, and food. No running from Larry if he shows up." He put a few meatballs on top of his potatoes. His voice hardly sounded like his own, and he hated it. Hated he'd brought this up at all. And yet, he couldn't stop himself from continuing.

"And with the new job, you won't be getting up so early. Class would be over." He finally lifted his eyes and looked straight at her. "And where does that leave us, Cassie?"

Could she hear all that he hadn't said? Had he revealed too much about how he felt about her, too soon?

So many questions plagued him, and the loudest one crowded out the others. Was he really in love with her already?

CHAPTER ELEVEN

Cassie didn't know how to answer Jon's question. She stared at him as he put garlic green beans and bacon on his plate, avoided the sweet potato hash, and moved over to the table where they'd shared breakfast so many times.

She blinked, trying to get her mind working again.

"You think I won't need you if I get the full-time job," she said.

He laughed, but it wasn't very happy. "Not at all," he said. "I already know you don't need me." His words hit her like nails shooting into her lungs.

"What?" she gasped.

"Cassie, you're a strong, independent woman. You don't *need* me."

She almost slammed the mashed potatoes onto her plate, adding the rest of her food before joining Jon at the table. Her fury felt as hot today as it had the day he'd sauntered into her kitchen and refused to leave.

"I'm risking everything to be with you," she said.

"I am too," he said, confusing her even more. He sighed

and leaned away from his plate. "Look, I have four classes left before I earn my degree in business management. Yours, the other one I'm in right now, and two business math classes."

Cassie held her fork in her hand, but she wasn't remotely interested in eating. "And you think you'll get kicked out of the university if our relationship is exposed."

"Possibly," he said. "I don't know. Just like you don't know what will happen to you if we're caught."

Cassie shook her head, hot tears pricking behind her eyes. "What are we doing here, Jon?" She'd refused to let herself classify their relationship as a mistake. Everything about being with him felt right, especially when they were together.

"I'm not sure, Cassie. You tell me one thing, but then hope for another. That's why I'm not sure what you really want." He forked up another bite of food and put it in his mouth. "And this is fantastic. You're a great chef. I hope you do get the job." He smiled at her, a quick movement of his mouth that she knew meant he was sorry he'd brought anything up at all.

She cut a meatball in half and scooped some potatoes onto it. "I do want to make a stable life for the twins here. The job would accomplish that. I just happen to have some... extenuating circumstances that require an escape plan."

"And I guess I just need to know if I'm part of the escape plan," Jon said.

Cassie couldn't believe he had to ask. She got up and rounded the table, dropping into a crouch in front of him. "Jon." She reached up and cradled his face in her hand, wishing she could express to him all the things she felt for him. "You've been my lifeline these past six weeks. The only reason I'm still sane since finding out Larry got out on parole. I do need you."

I will always need you.

She didn't say those words, but Jon was exceptionally

intelligent, and he leaned down and touched his mouth to hers for only a breath—so different from the way he kissed her as they laid together on the couch after breakfast.

In that simple, single touch, she felt loved, and she hoped she could accurately convey back to Jon that she loved him too.

She cleared her throat, confused again at what her life had become. She didn't want to give up her relationship with Jon. But she didn't want anyone to know about it. She wasn't sure if she loved Jon, as the thought of having her life so intertwined with his scared her endlessly. At the same time, she supposed it already was. She wanted the full-time job at the university, but the thought of making Forbidden Lake her permanent home added another layer of fear she didn't know how to deal with.

"My life is complicated," she said, straightening and moving around the table again. "I'm sorry about that."

"Hey, life would be boring without complications." Jon didn't look away from her. "Right?"

"I crave the boring life," she said, settling into her spot again. "Maybe one day, we'll have that. The cute, two-story house. The white picket fence. The house full of kids."

"Kids?" Jon asked, his eyebrows launching upward.

"Yeah," Cassie said. "You don't want kids?"

"Yeah, of course I do," he said. "I just didn't realize you did."

"I mean." Cassie tucked her hair behind her ear and smiled at her secret boyfriend. "Yeah."

"Yeah," he echoed back, and thankfully, the tension between them evaporated, leaving the rest of the evening open for the romance she'd hoped for.

❄

FRIDAY MORNING, SHE LEFT JON AT THE COTTAGE THE SAME way she always did. But this time, she'd gotten her good luck kiss and a boost of confidence before driving over to the college. She hoped her luck would hold out, because her confidence had fizzled before she'd even left the orchards.

She wore her best skirt suit, a cute little number in black, with a pale pink blouse beneath. She wore her hair down, curled nicely over her shoulders, and more makeup than she'd put on since her teen years.

Or maybe last year's interview. She carried a simple manila folder with her, the two letters of recommendation inside, along with her single-sheet résumé.

She sat in the lobby outside of Dr. Langstrom's office, a full fifteen minutes early. She did not pull out her phone. She didn't want to be on it when they came to get her. A good move, as only five minutes passed before the door opened and a man poked his head out. "Cassandra? We're ready for you."

Cassie put a smile on her face and stood, mentally commanding herself not to smooth down her clothes or appear nervous at all. "Hello, Doctor Zimmerman," she said. "I haven't seen you in a while."

"Retirement is keeping me busy," he said with a laugh.

"Are you sitting in on the interviews today?" She shook his hand and went inside the office when he waved for her to do so.

"Yes. Apparently, they need three people, and I got nominated."

Cassie moved forward into the office and found Dr. Langstrom sitting behind her desk, with the Dean of the Family and Consumer Sciences waiting in a chair beside her.

"Hello, Doctor Bean," she said, shaking the other man's hand as he partially stood. He wore thick, black-rimmed glasses and looked like an aged wombat. "Doctor Langstrom."

"Cassie, please sit down," she said instead of shaking Cassie's hand.

Cassie took the seat in front of the desk as Dr. Zimmerman took the other empty chair next to Dr. Langstrom. She adjusted her skirt to make sure it covered her knees, and then she balanced her folder on her lap.

"This is Cassandra Caldwell," Dr. Langstrom said. "She currently teaches our introductory culinary arts classes, including one to a group of twelve special needs students."

"Really?" Dr. Zimmerman asked. "That must have come after I left."

"Just last winter," Cassie said. "I do one class each term, so I'm in my fifth class."

"I'd like to come see it," he said, and panic paraded through Cassie with the strength of an elephant stampede. If anyone came to her special needs class, they'd see Jon— clearly not special needs.

"Anytime," she pushed out of her throat.

"Tell us why you want the full-time position," Dr. Langstrom said, her tone as crisp and no-nonsense as Cassie had ever heard it.

"Well." She took a deep breath, prepared to get personal. She mentioned how she took care of her twin half-brothers, as well as worked long hours in the very early morning at the bakery. "And with a full-time position here, I could focus on my teaching, provide good experiences for the students here, as well as have the resources I need to take care of my family."

She stopped talking, hoping she hadn't made everything about her, her, her.

"Do you feel like you have a good rapport with students?" Dr. Langstrom asked.

Cassie squirmed, but she managed to turn it into the motion of flipping open the folder. "I believe so, yes. I didn't have a lot of choices for my letters of recommendation, so I asked a student in my current course. She wrote me this."

She handed the letter across the desk to Dr. Langstrom. The department head glanced at it, but it wasn't nearly long enough to actually read what Molly had written. She handed the letter to the Dean, and he seemed to read it.

Dr. Langstrom launched into her next question. "You know we've had some trouble with professors getting romantically involved with their students. Have you ever been attracted to a student, Miss Caldwell?"

Her throat turned sticky, and Cassie had no idea what to say.

Time slowed to a crawl, and then it seemed to stop. In that moment, she knew she couldn't keep living a secret life with Jon, even if it was exciting. Even if she got a little thrill every time she parked in front of that cottage, knowing he'd be behind the door, waiting and ready to kiss her.

"I'm not much older than some of the students that go here," she said. "Some of them are older than I am. Have I ever been attracted to someone in one of my classes? Probably." That sounded true, because it was true.

Dr. Langstrom opened her mouth to say something else when Dr. Zimmerman said, "Do you have a sample course syllabus for any of the three extra courses you'd be teaching if you got the full-time professorship?"

Cassie swallowed and fumbled to pick her purse up from the floor at her feet. "Not in paper form, but I have a digital example I can show you." She looked at him expectantly, her eyebrows raised.

"Sure," he said, his voice kind and grandfatherly. Cassie hoped she could get this job, retire when she was older, and be as kind as him. She stood and leaned over the desk to show him the advanced appetizers course she'd put together.

It helped that the current professor kept his syllabus and course description online.

Several minutes later, the interview ended, and Cassie left the office on shaking legs. No one waited in the lobby, which meant they had timed the interviews so they applicants wouldn't see each other, or she was last for the day. The last one was unlikely, and as she waited for the elevator, her stomach roared with the want for food.

Her first class didn't start until noon on Fridays, so she had time for breakfast. Her first thought was to call Jon and ask him to meet her.

She scoffed at the very idea. She knew that deep down, she needed to get out of her relationship with him before things go too out of hand.

But what if they already are? she asked herself as the elevator doors slid open.

Josie Swartz stood there, wearing a deep navy pantsuit. She stepped out of the elevator and swept her eyes up and down Cassie's body. "You had an interview for the professorship too, didn't you." She wasn't asking. Cassie hadn't interacted with the food sciences teacher all that much, but neither one of them normally wore skirt suits or pantsuits to work.

"I did," Cassie said, switching positions with Josie. "Good luck." The car doors slid shut, and with them, her hopes deflated completely. Josie had much more experience than she did, and she'd been at Northwestern Michigan College for six years.

She'd deleted all her texts with Jon last night, as she usually did. She didn't want to bring up his name while still in the building, so she rode down to the bottom floor and walked out of the building.

Her phone buzzed as she turned onto Main Street, almost

like Jon knew she'd just left campus. But it was Kyle. *Made it to school safely.*

Relief sighed through her, and she sent a couple of heart emojis back to her brother, and then she pointed her car in the direction of Egg'lectic, the best breakfast joint in town. The parking lot was always full, and the waitresses quick with smiles and coffee.

Cassie got a spot at a table-for-two in the corner where she could see the whole restaurant as well as the street in front of the eatery. She ordered coffee and juice, as well as a bagel breakfast sandwich, with bacon, eggs, and kale.

She wished she were a normal woman, just hoping to get a better job to make a better life for her family. She could sip coffee after a stressful interview, and watch the Friday morning foot traffic saunter by, and send up a prayer or two.

Instead, Jon consumed her mind, and she knew she had to stop living inside a secret. Even if she didn't think their relationship was wrong. Even if they were both consenting adults and enjoyed each other's company. Even if he was the best man she'd ever called her boyfriend.

Even if she was falling in love with him.

So she pulled out her phone and sent him a text, hoping he could spare a few minutes that morning before he went into his shop.

CHAPTER TWELVE

J on had just pulled a T-shirt over his head when someone rang his doorbell. Goliath barked, a deep booming noise that made Jon want to cover his ears.

"Quietly," he said to the dog, whose whole body wagged as he ran to the door and back to Jon. He ran his hand through his still-damp hair and padded to the front door of his cabin-in-the-woods in his bare feet.

No one but mailmen came to his house and rang the doorbell. But it was after six-thirty at night, and he'd never gotten a package so late. Maybe Phoenix had made the trip in from his cabin, but he wouldn't have rang the doorbell. So Jon wasn't sure what to expect when he opened the door.

He found Cassie standing there in a sexy little skirt and blazer that rounded in all the right places. "Well, hello there." He leaned against the doorway. She glanced left and right, her nerves a scent on the air.

"Can I come in?" she asked. "Did you get any of my texts?"

"I sure didn't," he said. "And of course you can come in." He opened the screen door for her and stepped back. "I've been really busy today, finishing up a project I'm a week behind on. Once that was delivered, I grabbed dinner and came home. And now, I've just gotten out of the shower." He patted his jeans pockets and didn't find his phone. "I'm not entirely sure where my phone is right now. Maybe I left it at the shop."

Cassie came inside and Jon pushed the door closed behind her. She'd been to his house once before, and he'd practically made out with her right there in his kitchen, though his lips had never touched hers.

"How did the interview go?" he asked.

"Good," she said, walking away from him and into the kitchen. "Great. I got the job."

"You got the job?" He touched her elbow and gently turned her toward him, a smile pulling across his mouth. "That's so great."

But Cassie was crying—and not the happy kind of tears.

"Oh, okay," he said, backing up. "What's going on?"

"I can't live like this." She shook her head, her tears tracking down her cheeks. She swiped at them, sniffling and smearing her makeup. He didn't care. She was beautiful and perfect, no matter what she looked like.

"Like what?" he asked, though the stabbing pain through his chest told him what she'd meant.

"With the secrets. I can't do it."

"Hey." He took her hands in his. "We're consenting adults."

"It's still forbidden." She shook her head and backed up, out of his reach. "I need this job."

Jon wasn't sure if the air still had oxygen in it or not. His lungs screamed, and surely he'd suffocate in just a few seconds. "What are you saying?"

"We have to end this," she said, her voice growing

stronger. "Never speak of it. Maybe in a few months or a year—"

"A few months or a year?" Jon asked, his own emotions spiraling up and out of control. He shook his head. "No, Cassie. You don't have to do this."

"I've been thinking about it all day. There's no other solution." She wiped her face again and spun away from him. "And you really should've answered your stupid phone."

He clenched his teeth together to keep his retort inside. Her entertainment center had put him behind. So had the surprise he'd been designing and building for her, but he didn't want to tell her that.

"So this is your final decision." He leaned against the wall in the hopes that her breaking up with him was no big deal. "Can you at least look at me, please?"

She faced him, a perfect storm brewing in her eyes. "I'm so sorry."

"I'm in love with you," he said.

Her eyes widened, and she shook her head again. "No, you've always been enamored with the secrecy of us. You love that, not me."

"You're wrong." His jaw twitched, because he was clenching it so hard. But he wasn't going to say it again. He hadn't even meant to say it the first time.

"I have to go," she said, marching back toward the front door. "Move, Goliath. She stepped past the dog after partially kneeing him in her haste. She yanked open the door as a sob filled the air, and then she was gone.

Jon stood there and watched the front door drift back toward closed while his dog barked at something out in the darkness. Numb and unable to get his mind to work, he didn't have the heart to tell his dog to be quiet.

❄

Weeks later, the cherry blossoms were just starting to scent the air as Jon walked out to Phoenix's cabin. He'd gone several times a week since Cassie's sudden and final departure from his life.

He'd spent a lot of time walking along the shores of Forbidden Lake as winter thawed and spring dawned, awakening the trees and the birds. They sang to him, but not even the beloved sound of waves against the shore brought him happiness.

He wondered if he'd ever feel normal again, or if he'd continue to get up each morning, drink day-old coffee from the night before, and stumble into his shop. His designs were suffering, and every project was taking twice as long as it usually did. Sometimes three times as long. He'd lost several customers, and while he didn't really need the money, if he didn't have work to keep his mind occupied, he obsessed about Cassie.

Cassie, and how he could get her back.

Cassie, and the thrill of kissing her.

Cassie, and the way his whole heart ached for her.

No, the waves couldn't soothe away that kind of hurt.

"Knock, knock," he said as he entered the cabin through the front door.

"Hey," Phoenix practically yelled. He stood at the back door, and he tucked his shirt back into his pants as Jon entered. He'd definitely interrupted something, but he wasn't sure what. He scanned the cabin as if he'd find someone else there, but the only other person who ever came out here was the grocery delivery guy.

"How's the new cabin going?" he asked, yanking open the fridge and bending over to get something out of it, effectively concealing his face from Jon.

"Good enough," Jon said. "I just came from the site. I've got the foundation and framework done. It'll be ready by the tourist season." He accepted the can of soda from his brother and sank onto a barstool. "I'm not sure why Dad needs another cabin. We have thirty already."

"Well, it's one more, and that's another couple hundred dollars per night." Phoenix joined him at the other end of the bar. "Talk to Cassie?"

"Nope." Jon popped the P on the word and asked, "You seeing anyone?"

Phoenix started to laugh, but it held a note of falseness in it. "Are you serious?"

Jon shook his head, letting a smile drift across his mouth. "I guess not. Where would you meet someone, right? You never go anywhere."

"Hey, I go to work," he said.

"Name the last woman you talked to."

"Mom."

"That you weren't related to," Jon said as Phoenix answered.

They laughed again, and Jon stared down at his open soda can. "I miss her so much."

"You should just go over to her house. You know where she lives."

"No, I'm not doing that again." Jon had been through every scenario. Showing up at her house. Showing up during her office hours. Showing up to class. He'd done none of it. He couldn't stand to see her when she wore fear in her expression. Couldn't stand to talk to her with other students around. Couldn't afford to put her in danger of losing her new full-time job.

He wouldn't do any of those things. So his only option had been texting, and she'd shut him out completely. Not a single response. Cassie was headstrong and smart, and she'd probably blocked his number. That was what he would've done, simply so he wouldn't have to delete all her messages every night.

"Hang in there, bro," Phoenix said. "Even the heart heals with time."

"Yeah?" Jon asked. "Is yours almost whole then?"

Phoenix shrugged and lifted his drink to his lips. Jon took that as a no, and his fiancée had left years ago.

Years.

Jon wasn't sure he could live in this level of misery for that long, no matter how much diet soda he had. No matter how many projects he had to distract him. No matter how many miles he walked along the beach.

"Are you going to pass your class?" Phoenix asked. "You're not going anymore, right?"

"I still have an A," Jon said, his thoughts momentarily derailing toward Colton. Had the guy missed Jon at all? Would anyone, if he just stopped showing up to things the way Phoenix had?

He thought of the cottage Cassie had stocked with food and supplies. Jon could move in there, run his shop through texts and calls, maybe a video chat if absolutely necessary. He could get groceries delivered too. Live off the grid, the same way his brother did.

Phoenix got up and clapped Jon on the back. "Hang in there. You get up and you go to work and you talk to someone. It gets better."

"Who do you talk to?" he asked.

"You," Phoenix said with a smile. "I'm going to shower. Stay as long as you want." He glanced at his phone as he entered the hall, and Jon sat at the counter for a few minutes, listening to the spray of the shower.

He checked his phone again, insanely thinking that maybe Cassie had texted him in the twenty minutes since he'd last looked.

Nope.

Nothing.

From no one.

Jon didn't want to stay in this remote cabin, so he got up, yelled goodbye to his brother, and went back to the construction site along the lakeshore to get his truck. He couldn't go home, where only his giant mastiff waited for him.

So he grabbed the dog and went down the road to his parents' house. With any luck, they'd let him stay the night, even if they didn't like the way Goliath drooled.

CHAPTER THIRTEEN

Twenty-six days. That was how long it took for Jon to stop texting her. In the beginning, he'd sent dozens of messages per day. He'd called a few times too. As the time passed, the messages decreased, but they didn't stop until day twenty-seven.

Cassie cried again when she hadn't for a while.

Ten days, to be exact. She was now measuring everything in days. Sometimes hours. She hadn't seen Jon since breaking up with him in his cabin, and she was actually surprised he'd stopped coming to his culinary class on Tuesday and Thursday evenings.

Colton had asked about him, and Cassie had said she wasn't sure where he was and why he'd stopped coming. Sometimes a situation called for lying, she'd reasoned. She'd been so careful in her relationship with Jon, but she didn't feel like she'd ever flat-out lied. Even during the interview, she'd told most of the truth.

Was not telling the whole truth considered lying?

She wasn't sure, and she was tired of thinking about it. About Jon. About a solution that simply didn't exist. She couldn't have the full-time professorship *and* Jon, she simply couldn't.

"And you were stupid for thinking you could," she said to herself as she mixed yeast and milk together to make the shop's famous square glazed doughnuts.

"You are not going to believe what happened yesterday morning." Addy breezed through the back door, her arms laden with a box of baking ingredients. She deposited on the nearest stainless steel counter and faced Cassie, her eyes aglow.

"What?" Cassie asked. "Wait, let me guess." She took in Addy's sloppy ponytail and dazzling eyes with the dark bags underneath them. "You were out too late last night, because... Carlson asked you out."

"Yes!" Addy grabbed onto Cassie's doughy hands and jumped up and down. "And it was so awesome. Like magic. He took me out to Starlight with the Blossoms at one of the orchards, and there was music, and food, and dancing." She twirled in the kitchen, seemingly oblivious to the industrial space around her. "And then he kissed me, and said he'd been coming into the shop for months, trying to work up the courage to ask me out."

She giggled and pressed her eyes closed as she began to hum.

Cassie watched her, Addy's happiness and glee so infectious that Cassie couldn't help smiling. "So I'll get all the doughnuts done if you think you can focus long enough to do the tarts."

"Tarts," Addy said distantly, and Cassie focused on moving faster. Making fillings and frostings two or three at a time so she didn't have room to think about Jon and focus on how unhappy she was without the possibility of seeing him that day.

And now, she probably wouldn't hear from him either. She

waited until the last moment before bed before she deleted his texts, and it had cut deep last night that she hadn't had anything to erase.

Four hours, she told herself. She could get the shop stocked for the day in the next four hours. Then she'd get home, get the twins to school, and head in for her last regular classes of the semester. Next week was finals, and then she'd have a couple of weeks off before the summer term started.

She hadn't been out to the cottage in the woods in weeks and weeks, and she thought about taking the twins out of school and heading out there for the break between semesters. Maybe she just needed some free time and fresh air to get things clear in her head.

She told herself that, but she knew deep down that everything was already lined up in her mind. She couldn't be with Jon and keep it a secret, not if she wanted the full-time job at the university and a stable life for her brothers.

Family had won out over her heart again. Or maybe they were so integral to her heart that she'd chosen right. She wasn't sure. All she knew was that she existed in a fog that never lifted. Never allowed the sun to shine through. Never even allowed her a glimpse of hope ahead.

She did make it through the next four hours. She went home. She got the twins to school, and she went into her office at the college. The motions went by with the minutes, and then she could go home again.

One day became two, and then three, and by day four, Cassie thought she could go all day without checking her phone to make sure Jon hadn't messaged. But she was wrong, and she constantly checked just to make sure.

Another weekend came, and then March faded into April. She mourned the loss of the cottage in the woods, and she stole away after her last final to visit the place where she'd spent so much time.

In the middle of the day and with the cherry trees in full bloom now, she didn't think it likely that Jon would be around the orchards. She hadn't dared ask around about him, and besides, she didn't have anyone to ask. Addy was preoccupied with her new relationship with Carlson, and she'd never actually told the twins who she was dating.

The cottage was exactly as she remembered. Even the scent of bacon still hung in the air, and she wrapped her arms around herself as she took a deep breath of this place where she'd met Jon so often.

She loved the comfort that existed in this small room, and she craved the same serenity she'd enjoyed during her time with Jon. But she knew, even if they got back together, things wouldn't be the same. They never were, once priorities had been established. And Cassie had put him right where he'd feared she would.

Those blasted tears heated her eyes again, making them scratchy and reminding her of how tired she was. Maybe she could lay down just for a few minutes. The twins wouldn't be home from school for a couple of hours, and this cottage sat at the end of a road.

She grabbed a granola bar from her stock of snacks and wandered down the hall to the bedroom she'd claimed as her own. Her eyes immediately caught on the card propped against the lamp, and while she hadn't seen a lot of Jon's handwriting, she instinctively knew the envelope was from him.

Picking it up, she pressed it to her chest and collapsed onto the bed. Just having something he'd touched in her possession made her heart happier, and Cassie needed to find a way to fix her mistake.

There had to be something she hadn't thought of before. Some way for her to have Jon and her job and her family.

Somehow to honor the promise she'd made to her mother and honor the feelings in her heart.

She just couldn't see it. Couldn't find the right path....

She woke to pure darkness around her, and her phone buzzing somewhere nearby. Panic gripped her heart with icy fingers, and she scrambled up, her fingers flailing for the lamp switch. She knocked it sideways, grabbed onto it to steady it, and finally snapped the light on.

Groaning, she squeezed her eyes shut and shielded them with the back of her hand. Her phone stopped buzzing, and that sent another jolt of fear through her.

"Kyle," she whispered. "Lars." They'd be so worried about her. She hadn't told anyone where she was going, because she'd been planning to be home before them, as usual. But by the color of the sky, she was hours late.

She snatched her phone from the spot on the bed where it had fallen, and saw she'd missed nine calls, almost all of them from Kyle. One from Lars. And one from an unknown number.

She tapped on Kyle's name, as he'd just called, and when the line picked up, she heard Button yapping as she said, "I'm so sorry. I fell asleep, and I'm on my way—"

"He's here," Kyle said. "Don't come home, Cass! He's here." A snarl came through the line, more of Button's yapping, and then a sharp, cracking sound like the phone had hit the floor. Kyle continued to yell, but Cassie couldn't make out the words.

Fear turned into pure horror, because she knew who "he" was.

Larry had found them.

It hadn't even been six months, but Larry had found them.

Cassie's mind raced, and she couldn't seize onto one single thought in order to take action.

More scuffling came through the line, and then Lars's panicked whisper said, "We're still at home. He's been here for hours. He wants you here. Made us call you a bunch of times. Don't come back, Cassie. We're fine with him."

Then the line went dead.

A wail started in the back of her throat, and she stared at the phone, sure she'd just been pranked. In the cruelest way. But her phone showed that she'd been on the call for thirty-four seconds, and when the screen went dark, she flew into motion.

She dialed Willie in Chicago and barked, "Did you know Larry left the city?"

"What? No."

"Call the police. Give them an anonymous tip. Something. Anything to get them over to his place. Then tell them you know where I am, and you're worried about me and the boys."

"Cass, is he there?"

Tears blinded her, making it hard for her to get the door open. She struggled but finally got it, flying out into the night. "Yes," she said. "Hurry, Wills." She hung up and immediately placed another call.

This time to the last person on earth she wanted to bother, but the only person she knew would come, no questions asked.

"Hello?"

"Jon," she said. "Are you home? I need your help."

CHAPTER FOURTEEN

J on felt Cassie's panic all the way down in his own toes. His boots squelched in the mud as he walked through the orchard.

"I'm not home," he said. "I'm in the orchards." Before he'd even finished, she rushed on, her voice full of air as she panted.

"Larry's here. I wasn't home with the twins. I'm on my way there now."

"I'll come," he said without even thinking.

"Thanks. Gotta go." The line went dead before he could say anything else. He paused and looked at his phone. Had that just happened?

Her face—her oh-so-beautiful face—sat on his screen for a few seconds before darkening. So she really had called. His own adrenaline had spiked toward the treetops when he'd seen her name on his phone.

Larry's here.

Jon shoved his phone in his pocket and started running through the muck in the orchards. His father had wanted him to check on their picking huts and make sure they were ready for the summer, though the cherry harvest was still months away. It was amazing what damage Mother Nature could do during the fall and winter, and Jon had spent the day making repairs on two huts, and then making notes for a few more.

The sun had gone down, but twilight hadn't turned to night yet. He slipped in the mud, and he wished it hadn't been raining quite so much. Of course, everyone who owned a cherry orchard was happy for the rain. A lot of rain in the spring meant a lot of fruit in the summer. And more fruit meant more money.

His mind rotated, and when he reached solid ground, he pulled his phone out again and called 9-1-1.

"What's your emergency?" the operator asked.

"This is Jonathan Addler. My—" He couldn't call Cassie his girlfriend. They'd broken up seven weeks ago.

"Do you need help, sir?"

"Cassandra Caldwell just called me and said someone was in her house. Has she called in?"

"What's the address?" she asked. "I have you at 2419 Sunshine Shores Lane."

"Yes, I'm out at my family's cherry orchard. She's at her house." At least she was on the way there.

"Sir, do you know the address?"

Jon fumbled his keys and dropped them on the wet asphalt. He struggled to remember Cassie's address—somewhere he'd only been once and had followed her there in the first place.

"I think she's on Gunnison Road," he said. "I don't have the exact number."

"We'll send a unit down that way," she said.

Jon swiped the keys from the ground and got behind the wheel of his truck. "Okay, great, thanks." He hung up even as the operator started to ask him another question. He couldn't think and drive, and right now, he had to drive.

The ten-minute drive to town only took him five, and Jon made turn after turn until he came to Gunnison Road. It was this road, and her house sat down on the right—number three sixty-seven.

He committed it to memory even as he eased to a stop in front of the house. Something was very wrong here. Very, very wrong.

The front door was open a few inches, something Cassie would never allow. Light spilled out of the crack, and her car wasn't in the driveway. She surely had been closer than him, and he hadn't passed her on the way here.

He glanced up and down the street, but it looked like all was well. No one stood on their front lawn, gossiping about what had happened at this house.

But something had happened.

Jon got out of the truck, pulled up his recent calls in case he needed to dial into emergency again quickly, and approached the house cautiously. He wanted to call for Cassie, but he didn't dare. He wasn't sure his voice would work anyway.

"Sir," a man said in a firm, authoritative voice, and Jon spun back toward the sidewalk.

A police car had pulled up behind him, and two officers had gotten out. "Do you live here?" one of them asked.

"No," he said, clearing his throat. "I'm Jonathan Addler. I called in to nine-one-one for my friend, Cassie. She lives here." He turned back to the house. "There's something wrong here. Her car isn't here, and I know she was here."

He couldn't believe she hadn't been home with the twins when Larry had shown up. And how had Larry left Chicago already? He wasn't supposed to leave the city for another two months, and he was risking a lot to come to Forbidden Lake.

That's because he's not going back to Chicago, Jon thought. He was going to take those boys and run, and while Jon had only met them once, he knew how much they meant to Cassie. Knew she'd promised her mother she'd take care of them.

"Stay here," the other officer said. "All the way back by the car, Jon."

Jon looked at the guy, realizing it was Morgan Quinn, a friend from all the way back in high school. Jon nodded at him and retreated back to his own car.

He heard the officer speak to Morgan and point to something on the front steps, and then he nudged open the front door and let it settle all the way open, revealing more of the house. They inched inside, and each moment felt agonizingly slow.

Cassie wasn't here. The twins weren't here. Larry wasn't here.

So where were they?

He called Cassie, the way her phone rang and rang doing nothing to settle him. He held his device against his side and listened, hoping to hear her phone ringing from nearby. But the neighborhood was deathly silent.

He hung up and walked toward the house. The grass looked a little rumpled near the bottom of the steps, like a few people had tread there one right after the other as they exited from the house in a herd.

Going up the steps slowly, his eyes easily landed on the spots of blood on the cement on the porch. His breath stuck in his lungs. Whose blood was that? Had Cassie done something to Larry, taken the twins, and disappeared?

Jon's whole heart wailed, and while he hadn't spoken to her in a while, he'd been making plans. After this semester ended, and after he delivered her new entertainment center, he'd ask her out again. Try again.

He wouldn't be her student then, and everything would be fine.

His gaze caught on a pen lying on the porch too. He bent

down to get a closer look, knowing he shouldn't pick it up but wanting to so badly.

"No." He groaned as he saw the J clearly written there on the cement. Well, clearly if he got six inches away and squinted. He knew that J was for him.

The whole message read *J – room 615*

"The college," he breathed, straightening. "Guys. Morgan," he called into the house. "She's at the college." He leapt down the stairs and ran for his truck.

"Jon," Morgan called after him. "Wait."

He couldn't wait. He had to go. He had to get to her now.

Morgan caught him before he could drive off. "Where is she?" he asked, glancing toward the house as his partner came down the steps. "Something happened inside that house. There's blood in a few places, and furniture upside down."

Jon's nerves buzzed with adrenaline. With pure fear for Cassie and her brothers. He hopped out of his truck. "You guys drive. I'll tell you what I know on the way over to Northwestern Michigan College."

"What—?"

"Now," Jon barked. "No time for questions." He darted over to the police car and got in the back while everyone else loaded into the front. "Okay, get the lights on and get us there fast. Here's what I know."

He detailed what Cassie had told him about Larry and her brothers over the couple of months they'd been together. He told them about her phone call to him while he was in the orchard, and the message he'd found on the front porch.

Hal, Morgan's senior partner, called for additional units to go to the house to secure the crime scene, as well as for the college.

"An emergency call just came from Northwestern Michigan," his dispatch came back.

Everything went silent in the car, and Hal somehow made the already speeding car go faster.

"Who called it in?" Jon managed to ask.

Hal repeated the question through his radio.

"A Barbara Langstrom," dispatch said. "She said she's hurt with a broken arm, and there's a man with a knife with one of her teachers and a pair of teenage boys. They're barricaded in one of the kitchens there."

"Room six-fifteen," Jon said. "It's the kitchen where Cassie teaches all of her classes." Dread filled his stomach, and he leaned back against the seat behind him. "And Barbara Langstrom is the department head over the culinary arts program."

"She's still alive," Morgan said, turning toward Jon. "So Jon, let's do this the right way. You can't go running in there, trying to save your girlfriend."

"She's not my girlfriend," he said automatically—and while he'd been prepared to tell that lie, he'd never had to. Not even this time.

Morgan's eyebrows went up, but he turned around without saying anything else. Hal got them to the college, and Jon directed him where to park to be as close to the kitchens as possible. "There's her car," he said pointing. Another one— a fancier one—sat next to it.

Hal pulled right up onto the sidewalk as if he'd ram the brick building, coming to a sudden stop that had Jon thinking he'd have whiplash.

A woman stumbled toward them, and both officers flew from the car. Jon had never met Cassie's boss, but Cassie had told him all about the woman.

"Stay here with Jon," Morgan said, helping Barbara Langstrom into the backseat where Jon still sat. He didn't close the door all the way before turning and sprinting back to the door where Hal stood pressed against the side of the brick.

"Are you okay if I leave?" he asked her.

She nodded, but her face was one of pain and panic.

"Was Cassie alive?" he asked. "The boys?"

"Yes," she said, her voice rusty and hoarse. "There's a huge man with them. Angry. Waving a knife. I tried to stand up to him, but he pushed me down." She cradled her arm. "Cassie said the papers were in her office."

Jon had one leg out of the car when he paused. "Papers?"

Barbara nodded. "I don't know what she meant. I didn't know she was in trouble."

He wanted to get inside and help her so badly, but still he didn't move. "You knew she took care of her half-brothers, right?"

Barbara nodded again.

"Well, that huge guy is their dad, and he just got out of prison in January. First day of class, actually." He got out of the cop car and faced the building. In the distance, more sirens could be heard. Whatever Cassie and Larry were going to do, they'd need to do it quickly.

"I'm going in," he said. "Are you sure you're okay here?"

"I'll come with you."

"No," he said. "You're already hurt."

"I know how to get in the kitchen through another door." Barbara got out of the car too, and while she cradled her arm, she walked with purpose. Jon saw blood smeared on the door handle, the walls, and even a glass display case as they went by.

The hallway inside the building was only lit by the emergency lights, casting eerie shadows onto the walls.

"How do you know Cassie?" she whispered.

Jon took a moment to think before he whispered back. "I'm a student in one of her classes."

"This way," Barbara said, turning left when Jon would've continued straight. There was a handprint there—almost a perfect piece of art. Jon looked at it for a moment, his stomach filling with rocks. He had to find Cassie right now. Do something to get her and the boys away from Larry.

Barbara turned right then left again, and came to two doors at the dead-ended hallway they ended up in. "That's the kitchen." She nodded to the first door. "And that's a back entrance to her office." She looked at the door several feet down, at the very end of the hall. "We never use these doors. They're probably locked."

Jon tried the one closest to him, the one that would take him into the kitchen near the front, where Cassie stood to teach and demonstrate. The handle went down, but the door stayed stubbornly closed.

"Yep, locked," he whispered. He eyed the other door. No way she'd left that door unlocked. Knowing her, she'd locked it and then boarded it up. She wouldn't want anyone sneaking up on her.

Jon had only been in her office on the first day of class, and he certainly hadn't been looking for doors at that time. He drew in a deep breath and stepped past Barbara.

"One way to find out."

CHAPTER FIFTEEN

"I t's here somewhere," she said, pulling another file of papers out of her cabinet. Her head hurt where Larry had hit her, but at least the blood had congealed enough to stop tracking down the side of her face. She'd lost count of how many times she'd wiped it, and she'd been sure to touch everything she could.

She hoped Dr. Langstrom would notice the almost complete handprint she'd put on the wall that led to the back entrances to the kitchen and her office. She hadn't been able to get away from Larry long enough to unlock that kitchen door, and she felt horrible for putting Dr. Langstrom in danger in the first place.

She'd had an emergency flip phone in the glove compartment of her car. On the way here, amidst the chaos of claiming she needed a napkin for her bleeding head wound, Kyle had managed to get the phone as well as pass a tissue to her.

The phone had exactly one number in it—Dr. Langstrom's. She was all Cassie had when they'd first come to

Forbidden Lake, and only putting in one number made it easy to make a call without having to look at the phone.

So Kyle had, and then Cassie had made a big deal about where she was taking Larry and the boys, and how long it was until they arrived, and that surely the cops, whom she'd already called would be there.

Dr. Langstrom may not have had all the pieces, but she'd been at the college when Cassie had pulled up with everyone else. The older woman had been shocked to see Cassie being manhandled by a thug three times as big as her, but she'd squared her shoulders and said they couldn't go inside.

Larry wasn't taking no for an answer tonight, and poor Dr. Langstrom's arm had snapped as soon as she'd hit the ground.

Cassie pushed against the desire to throw up, that horrible cracking sound of Dr. Langstrom's bone still echoing in her head.

"Hurry up," Larry growled from his position next to the door that led into the kitchen. Lars had already unlocked the one beside the filing cabinet, which she usually kept locked and stored files in front of. But Kyle had immediately hauled all those boxes out and started going through them, looking for the legal paperwork Larry wanted.

Their birth certificates. The legal guardianship papers. Their social security cards.

Cassie actually kept the originals at home, but she had copies in every runaway bag—also still at home or at the cottage or the trunk of her car.

And a set here in her office, that she couldn't seem to find. She knew where they were, but she and the boys had been through every scenario she'd been able to think of. And this one would hopefully continue to go as they'd practiced.

The boxes were between them and Larry. The door was unlocked. Now she just needed him to be distracted enough that they could fly out the door and into the kitchen next door. They'd never practiced, as doing so had scared Lars too much.

A man yelled something from the kitchen, and Larry locked his gaze in that direction.

"Go," Cassie hissed, and Kyle didn't waste another second. He pulled open the door and he and Lars were gone in an instant. Cassie followed them, not taking even a moment to look back.

But there was nowhere to go, and she collided with a couple of other bodies in the hall.

"Cassie," Jon said, and relief flowed through her. Except him being there was causing a problem—there wasn't room for her to get fully out of the office and close the door.

"Move," she whispered, and it felt like years but was only seconds before she was in the hall with the door to the office closed behind her. "Come on," she hissed. "We can't stay here."

She'd taken one step when a bellow sounded from the office. "Go, go." Surprise darted through her, only adding to the cacophony of emotions surging in her bloodstream, when she saw Dr. Langstrom in the hall.

They rounded the corner just as the door crashed into the wall, and Larry said, "You can't outrun me."

Cassie knew that. Oh, she knew that.

"Right," she hissed to Jon, and he opened the door into the adjoining kitchen, waiting until they'd all gone by him before going in and closing the door. He fumbled with the lock while Larry pounded on it, yelling obscenities from the other side.

"Over here," she said to the boys, guiding them in the dark while watching Jon struggle with the door. If he got hurt, she'd never forgive herself. "In the pantry. There's another door. Remember, left, right, left."

She turned back to help Dr. Langstrom and had just

gotten her in the pantry when the door practically exploded in on Jon.

"Jon," she screamed, running back toward him.

Larry came through the door, and it was her very night-mare personified. He stood so tall, with shoulders that were impossibly wide. He'd worked out for the twelve years he was in prison, because he was two hundred and ninety pounds of muscle. With a knife.

Jon scrambled backward, grabbing onto a drawer handle as he stood. He rattled around in there until he came up with a pair of tongs, which he held up as if they could do some real damage to Larry and his eight-inch blade.

In fact, Larry laughed. The sound made Cassie's blood turn to ice, but she reached into the drawer and pulled out the first thing her fingers curled around. A can opener.

She met Jon's eyes and faced Larry. "You can't take my brothers," she said, feeling brave for the first time since she'd broken up with Jon. And what a cowardly thing that had been. Shame raced through her, but she couldn't change the past nor deal with that relationship right now.

"They're my sons," he growled.

"The court granted custody and guardianship to me," she said. "And you'll be going right back to prison, because you've violated your parole by leaving Chicago."

"I'm never going back," he said, so much hatred streaming from his eyes that Cassie wondered what his plan had been. Cross the border, probably. Get new identities in Canada with the legal documents he wanted so badly.

Larry took a step forward, and Jon and Cassie fell back one. Jon opened another drawer and glanced inside it. "Cans," he whispered as Larry continued to glower.

Cassie wondered how long they could hold him off. She'd never been great at softball, and throwing something and having it hit her target almost never happened. She pulled open the drawer on her side as they took another step backward. It had silverware in it.

Plenty of things to throw.

"There's two cops here," Jon said, not trying to keep his voice down. "Let's start yelling and throwing everything we can."

"I can hear you," Larry said.

Cassie didn't wait to hear what Jon's response to him was. She launched her handheld can opener at Larry, as surprised as anyone when it hit Larry on his right cheek. He yelped, and his hands went right to his face.

She grabbed a handful of forks and spoons and threw them too, screaming at the same time.

Jon threw can after can of sweetened condensed milk, each one hitting their mark until Larry went down to his knees, his whole face seemingly bleeding.

"Go, Cass," Jon said as the door to the kitchen opened and two cops came in. "Morgan," he called. "He's up here. Hurt. The knife went skidding somewhere." Jon pushed her away from Larry as the cops ran toward him. A moment later, two more entered, weapons drawn.

She detoured over to the pantry to get her brothers, and she drew them both into her arms, saying, "It's over. They've got him. We're fine. We're fine."

We're fine. Her mind repeated it endlessly, and when Jon wrapped his arm around her shoulders, the tears came.

She clung to her brothers, and Jon encircled them all, shushing them and whispering that it was all okay now. He pressed his lips to her temple more than once, until finally the cops came into the pantry to officially declare that Larry wasn't in the building anymore.

Jon secured his hand in hers, and Cassie was thankful for the anchor. He insisted on going with her, and she refused to let Kyle and Lars out of her sight, so the four of them ended up with a couple of cops, where she answered question after question.

Kyle and Lars did too, and in the next room over, Dr. Langstrom did too.

By the time she was finished and the cops said she could go home, Cassie's exhaustion prevented her from even moving.

"I'm driving," Jon said. "Keys, please."

"Jon."

"Do not argue with me," he said. "You guys okay with me driving?" He looked at Kyle and Lars, who both betrayed her by nodding.

Cassie handed him her keys, never wanting to get back in that car again. But she walked past Dr. Langstrom, with her hand in Jon's, and she got in the passenger seat of her own car. The whole vehicle smelled tinny, like blood, and she closed her eyes.

Jon bought them all food at a drive-through, and then he set off down the road toward the orchards. He took them all the way to the cottage, locking them all inside.

He helped Kyle and Lars find their room, showed them where their pj's were, and then came out to the living room where Cassie had collapsed on the couch.

Kneeling in front of her, Jon stroked her hair off her face. "Let's get you cleaned up, sweetheart."

He was so kind to her, even after she'd cut him out of her life these past several weeks. After she'd chosen everything else over him.

She started crying, which only made her head hurt worse than it already did.

"Don't cry," he whispered, leaning down and touching his lips to hers. "I'll be right back."

He got up and went into the kitchen, the water turning on a few seconds later. When he returned, he pressed a hot cloth to her head, cleaning up the blood on the side of her face and examining the head wound on her right side, a few inches above her ear.

He'd heard everything that had happened—how Larry had hit her the moment she'd walked in the door. She'd caught sight of upturned furniture, and Kyle had told her through his tears that Larry wanted all their legal documents.

Cassie had thought fast, despite her injury, and she'd immediately told him she didn't keep any of that at the house. He'd torn a few things apart and hadn't found them, so Larry had believed her, and they'd all gone off to the college.

"There you go, Cass," he said. "All cleaned up. Let's get you to bed."

In another situation, she might have thought he was coming on to her, but not tonight. He helped her down the hall and pulled some pajamas out of the dresser drawer. "You change, and I'll come say good-night."

Cassie watched him start toward the door, and she said, "Jon, wait."

He turned back to her, his dark eyes shining with hope and...love. He'd said he was in love with her, and looking into his eyes, she could see it. Feel it.

A fresh wave of emotion hit her, and she gestured for him to come back over to her. He did exactly that, sweeping her into his strong arms. "It's okay," he whispered. "You're safe here."

"Don't go," she whispered back. "I can't stay here alone."

"Kyle and Lars are here."

"Please, stay." She nuzzled her face deeper into his neck, breathing in the uniquely masculine scent that belonged to Jon. Part pine and part cherry blossom, he smelled like safety.

"Of course I'll stay," he whispered back.

"I'm so sorry," she said. "I was so scared, and I didn't know who else to call."

"You can always call me." He stepped back and cleared his throat. "I'll just be outside while you change."

She waited until he reached the door to say, "Jon, do you think we can make it?"

He turned back to her but didn't return to her. "Me and you?" He smiled, one of those sexy, soft smiles than Cassie loved. "Yeah, Cass. I've always known me and you are going to make it."

"You have?"

He nodded, ducked his head, and slipped out the door.

In that moment when the bedroom door clicked closed behind him, Cassie knew she was in love with Jon. Her forbidden little crush had blossomed into full-blown love.

She hurried to change into her pajamas, and then she opened the door to find him sitting on the floor just outside her bedroom.

"Hey." He got to his feet and reached for her. "I don't know if you're ready to get back together or not. It doesn't really matter. I know you'll have a lot to deal with for a while. But you should know my feelings for you haven't changed."

She gazed up at him. "Mine have."

His eyes glassed over and his jaw tightened. He looked away from her, a sigh making his shoulders slump.

"I don't know what will happen tomorrow," she said. "Or the next day. But I do know I'm in love with you, and if you're by my side, I can handle anything."

Jon's gaze flew back to hers. He searched her face, that hope and love and joy filling his expression. "I love you too." He dipped his head, and then paused. "Can I kiss you now?"

Cassie answered by lifting onto her toes and pressing her lips to his in the sweetest kiss of her life.

CHAPTER SIXTEEN

Jon woke when Cassie touched his shoulder. He opened his eyes, still soft-minded from sleep, and smiled at her. "Hey, beautiful."

She perched on the couch near his chest. "We have a problem."

Jon pushed himself up, his back a bit kinked from sleeping on this horrific couch. "Another one?"

"Doctor Langstrom texted me. She said she's glad I'm okay, and that she could help. But then she said we needed to talk about my relationship with my student." She turned the phone toward Jon, but he didn't need to take it and read the messages from her boss.

"It's my fault," he said. "She asked me how I knew you, and I said I was your student."

"I don't even care," she said, letting the phone drop back to her lap. "I'm not going to choose the job over you again."

Jon's whole soul felt like someone had inserted the sun into his chest. "Is that so?"

She glanced at him, matching her smile to his. "Yeah,

that's so." She curled into his chest, and he wrapped her in his arms.

Jon held her for a few minutes, just enjoying the way she breathed with him and how easy it was to be with her. "So what now?" he finally asked.

"I've always wanted to open my own restaurant," she said. "Maybe I should just do that."

"I know a guy who can help you fix a place up, if you need it," he whispered, placing a kiss behind her ear.

She cuddled deeper into his chest, and that was how Kyle found them when he came out of his bedroom a few minutes later.

"Hey," Jon said, nudging Cassie so she'd disentangle herself from him. They both got up from the couch, and Kyle moved over to Jon and hugged him. Surprise pulled through Jon, and he didn't quite know what to do except for pat the teen on the back.

"Thank you for helping us last night," Kyle said, backing up and wiping his hand down his face. His complexion might have been a little ruddier than before, and Jon didn't see any tears. "Is there anything for breakfast out here?"

Jon couldn't help a quick chuckle. "I don't think you know Cass if you have to ask that."

Kyle smiled too. "You're right. I forgot for a minute who I was dealing with."

"Hey," Cassie said defensively. "Go find the peanut butter cereal you like, before I throw it all out." She smiled at Kyle, and he hugged her too on his way into the kitchen.

"I'm going to go check on Lars," she said. "He's the more sensitive of the two, and he'll want to talk through everything."

"All right," Jon said, a little nervous to be left alone with Kyle. Why, he wasn't sure. Probably because he had very little experience with teenagers, and he wasn't sure how Kyle felt about his sister dating Jon.

Cassie stopped to give him another kiss. "And then we can get ready and go over to see Doctor Langstrom in the hospital."

"She's texting you about university business from the hospital?"

"She's the Eagle, remember?" Cassie trailed her fingers down his arm and then left to go check on Lars. Kyle sat at the counter, eating, and Jon leaned back into the couch and closed his eyes again, happiness streaming through him despite the storms of the past twenty-four hours.

HIS JOY AND CONTENTMENT HAD FLED BY THE TIME THEY pulled back into the parking lot outside the hospital. Jon drove, and after he turned off his truck, they still both sat in the cab, staring out the windshield.

He wasn't sure what was running through Cassie's mind, but he could see everything from the night before as clearly as if it were still happening, even though the hospital sat on the other side of town from the college.

"I can't go back to that house," she said.

"I'll get my brothers to help, and we'll get you moved out." He finally stopped staring at the double doors in front of him. "Okay, Cass? You can move into the cabin permanently."

"I can't do that either," she said. "I'll find us somewhere else. I have a break between semesters." She pressed her lips together and closed her eyes. "I mean, I have a break until I find a new job." She unbuckled her seat belt. "Let's go."

Jon got out of the truck and took her hand in his when she met him at the front of the vehicle. "Are you sure you want me to come? Maybe you can deny everything. I could've just been overly...worried. Or something."

She shook her head. "I don't want to deny it." She paused and looked up at him, those dark eyes as mesmerizing now as they had been that first day in class. "I want us to be together. It's better to tell the truth, come what may."

Come what may. His mother had said that so much growing up, and a rush of affection for Cassie streamed through him. He kissed her quickly, wishing they had more time and more privacy for what he really wanted to do. "All right, then. Let's go."

They entered the hospital and went up to the second floor, where they found Dr. Langstrom sitting in a chair in her room, her eyes out the window.

"Hello, Doctor Langstrom," Cassie said, drawing the older woman's attention from whatever she was watching outside.

"Cassie, come in." She turned all the way toward them, her gaze stalling on Jon and then dropping to their interlocked fingers.

There wasn't anywhere for him to sit, and he felt seven shades of awkward as Cassie took the only other chair and faced her boss.

"I'm so sorry to involve you," she said. "You were the only person I knew when we first got to town, and I hadn't updated my alert system."

Barbara blinked, the surprise evident in her expression. "You're a smart woman, Cassie."

"I'm just trying to keep my brothers safe." She drew in a deep breath. "At this point, I'd usually leave town. Find another job somewhere several hours away, and start over. But the twins like it here." She glanced up at Jon. "And I want to stay here."

Warmth filled him, and he smiled down at her. He didn't

want to admit that until that moment, he hadn't been one-hundred percent sure if she'd stay in Forbidden Lake or not.

She exhaled. "But, as you obviously figured out, I'm seeing a student. Even though he's older than me, and we're both adults, I know the school's policy. So I'll be resigning, effective immediately."

Barbara swallowed and nodded. "You'll still get your severance if we do it that way." She looked at Jon. "And you won't lose your credits."

"Was that a possibility?" he asked, a flicker of nerves dancing through him.

"Anything is a possibility," Barbara said, her voice taking on a sharper edge. "But there's been no complaints made, and I don't see any evidence of grade tampering, and well." She smiled, but it was fleeting and nowhere near warm. "I think we've all been through enough."

Cassie nodded, sniffling a little. "I will miss teaching for you."

"You were a great professor," she said. "Come by my office on Monday, and fill out the resignation paperwork, would you?"

"Of course."

Barbara stood. "And if you two could help me downstairs and perhaps give me a ride home...." She wore vulnerability in her eyes now, and Jon hooked his arm through hers.

"Of course, Barbara," he said, leaving Cassie to grab the older woman's bag. "You know, I have a friend who's got to be close to your age."

"Oh, stop it," she said with a light laugh. "I'm much too old to start seeing someone."

"You're never too old to have someone in your life who cares about you," Jon said, glancing over Cassie's shoulder. "Right, Cass?"

"Absolutely right," she said, coming up beside them once they left the hospital room.

"I have cats," Barbara said. "And they're as demanding as any man would be. I'm fine."

Jon chuckled, his earlier contentment returning. "If you say so. But let me know if you want Sherman's number. He works on our crew at the orchards, and he's older, single dad of two grown kids, pretty handsome if I do say so...." He let his voice trail off when Cassie started laughing, and a beam of light shone right into Jon's soul with the sound.

He held onto that heat and energy while he drove Barbara home and helped her inside. While he took Cassie back to the cottage, where Kyle had put a couple of pizzas in the oven for dinner. And long after everyone had gone to bed, and Jon lay on the hard couch for the second night in a row, he experienced the light that his love for Cassie had brought into his life.

Or maybe he felt like he'd been dancing on clouds for the afternoon and evening because of Cassie's love for him.

She'd given up her job—the one thing she'd been desperate to hold onto—for him. She was going to stay in town and rebuild her life instead of running to a different place and starting over.

She was doing all of that, because she loved him.

Jon smiled, closed his eyes, and hoped the future for the two of them would always be full of this happiness and light that he felt in his heart right now.

CHAPTER SEVENTEEN

Cassie sighed as she dusted her hands off and dismounted from the ladder. "I think I'm done," she said to Jon, who worked in a nearby cherry tree. "I have to go in to the restaurant this afternoon and run a staff meeting. Then I'm cooking all night."

"Yeah," Jon said. "I'm bringing the twins at ten. Birthday dinner and cake after you close."

She smiled up at him, the plans they'd made for Kyle and Lars always at the forefront of her mind. He came down the ladder too, his bucket brimming with ripe cherries. Her life had changed so much in the past three months. Well, in the past seven months, actually. Since she'd met Jon in January.

He kissed her and picked up her cherry-filled bucket. "Things okay at the restaurant?" he asked.

They'd opened last month, and while business had been steady, Cassie was barely breaking even. She'd found another cute little house, this one on the outskirts of town, closer to the cherry orchards than downtown. She had great neighbors to help with the twins, but Jon had taken over that duty.

School was out now, and while she worked, they came out

to the orchards to work or went to his carpentry shop to hang out. They'd had picnics on the beach and taken day-trips up the coast to the sandier parts of the lakeshore.

"Things are okay," she said, because they were. No, she wasn't getting rich quickly. But she had a place to live, Larry was back in prison, and she and Jon were getting along great.

"I've been thinking," he said as they walked beneath the tree limbs. Everything in the orchards looked the same to her, but Jon never got lost. She loved the serenity of the trees, and of being with him.

"Oh, boy." She laughed and bumped him with her hip.

"So your hostess stand is almost done," he said. "And the restaurant is open. And harvest season will be over soon. After that, I was thinking maybe we'd have time to start planning a wedding."

Cassie's breath stalled in her lungs. "Jon, are you serious?"

"Have I ever given you the impression that I don't want to marry you?" He scoffed and shook his head. "You're the one who's been holding us back. After we get settled in our new house, Jon. After the restaurant is open, Jon. After the harvest is over, Jon." He spoke in a pitched-up voice, almost mocking her.

"I do not sound like that." She laughed, because she probably did.

He laughed too, switched one bucket to his other hand, and put his arm around her waist. "I love you, Cass. And you love me. And I love the boys. We should be a family."

Cassie had thought about marrying Jon, sure. But he was right—she did always push it away, or let something else crowd out the thought. She just didn't have the mental space to deal with it...until now.

"So come with me," he said, setting their buckets down next to the tree at the end of a row. He took her hand in his and walked faster now.

"Where are we going?"

"To the beach, of course," he said, smiling. "It's the most romantic place to get engaged."

Her heart floundered in her chest, but she kept up with him while he led her to the beachfront. In July, with the sun shining down, the beach was a popular place. Families and couples had staked their claim on patches of sand, and the lake sent gentle waves rolling ashore.

Jon drew in a deep breath. "I love this lake."

"You've told me about fifty times," she said.

He chuckled. "All right." He stepped in front of her and dug into his pocket. "And I love you, Cassandra Caldwell. Even though you tried to kick me out of your class. Even though you never let me come over to your house. Even though you tried to walk away from me. I always hoped, and then I knew, that we'd be together."

He held up a ring that glinted in the bright sunlight and dropped to both knees right there in the sand. "Will you marry me?"

A swell of joy as large as a tsunami rushed through her, and she moved her eyes from the ring to his. "Of course I will." She bent down and took his face in both of her hands, the way he'd done the first time he kissed her, and matched her mouth to his.

This kiss was just as explosive and just as meaningful as their first secret, forbidden kiss in the cottage.

Because this time, she was kissing the man she loved and her fiancé.

"I love you." He got to his feet, slipped the ring on her finger, and kissed her again. "I do miss having this delicious secret between us," he murmured. "Maybe we can keep our engagement quiet for a while. Just something we only know."

Cassie looked into his sparkling eyes, hoping she and Jon

always had a secret just the two of them shared. "Good idea," she said.

"Great," he said, kissing her again, the sound of the waves the perfect background music for their new lives together.

Read on for a sneak peek of **HIDDEN IN THE WOODS**, featuring Phoenix, Jon's brother, and his reclusive ways in the woods.

SNEAK PEEK! HIDDEN IN THE WOODS
CHAPTER ONE

Phoenix Addler stood in the kitchen of his cabin, the only sound the dishwasher behind him humming away on that week's dishes. Maybe two week's worth. He didn't exactly use a lot of dishes, though he could cook just fine.

He wasn't walking over to his job in the state forest today, which was only more walking. Hiking, he supposed, as he led groups out along the trails to hidden lakes and picture points. He didn't mind the tours he did a few times a week. They got him together with other human beings, which admittedly, Phoenix didn't do a whole lot of on days he didn't have tours.

It had been a mild winter so far, but the weathermen were predicting snow in the next few days. Then the ground would be frozen, and that fence post that the last storm had dislodged wouldn't get fixed for a few more weeks.

It wasn't that Phoenix wanted the fence between the Addler family property, where he lived right in the tippy corner of, and the Forbidden Lake State Forest. Only that he didn't want anyone coming onto his land, and he liked knowing how far he could go before he "arrived" at work.

That, and the Michigan Department of Natural Resources was looking for any ticky-tack reason to swoop in with another infraction against him. Okay, not the whole department. Just their top agent in the region, and Phoenix's teeth clenched harder at the mere thought of having to deal with the state agency again.

His family owned this land, and they didn't have to develop it. His father was very careful about how many new cherry trees they planted each year, having taught Phoenix and all his siblings that the care of the earth was the most important.

So each year, they planted fifteen to twenty new trees, and his father babysat them as if they were humans. His father's love for his orchards stemmed from Phoenix's grandfather's careful attention to their crop, citing the trees as family members without names.

Phoenix had gone to college in wildlife management, because he too believed that living things deserved respect.

So he'd reset the fence post today and get the fence back in place. That way, none of the animals that lived in the state forest would cross over onto the Addler Family land.

His phone buzzed as he shrugged into his leather jacket, and he saw a text from Rick, his boss at his second job. *You up for chopping today?*

Phoenix zipped up his jacket and reached for his gloves before tapping out. *Sure. This afternoon?*

Come out to farm eight whenever you can, Rick answered, and Phoenix let the conversation die there. He usually didn't need to say a whole lot to get his point across, and Rick knew his text had gone through.

Phoenix liked the lumberjack work almost more than the hiking and wildlife care at the state park. But lumberjacking wasn't full-time and didn't provide benefits. He also needed a car to get there, and he didn't own one of those either.

He hadn't consciously tried to reduce his footprint on the earth; it had sort of just happened when he'd moved into this cabin. He paid all his bills online, did all of his shopping online, enjoyed grocery delivery, and he could walk down the lane where all the other family cabins sat in a long, straight row.

Truth be told, his brother Jon usually came to get him for Sunday meals. And if Jon wasn't using his truck today, Phoenix could borrow it to get out to the tree farm where Rick operated his firewood business.

But he'd deal with all of that after setting the fence post. It had been dry and warm for the past few days, so he left his gloves in the lean-to beside the house and grabbed the shovel. He couldn't imagine working from an office, or even inside a building. He was grateful for his cabin, which provided shelter from heat and cold, but he'd endured college by the skin of his teeth.

So much sitting. Not enough doing.

Phoenix was definitely a do-er, and he set his phone on the properly set fence post and said, "Call Brother Jon."

His phone repeated back to him, "Calling Brother Jon," and the ringing came through the line as Phoenix probed around the hole where the fence post had been.

"Hey, Phoenix," Jon said. "What's up?"

"I need a truck to get over to chop today. What are you doing?"

"I'm at the shop."

"So I'll call Dad." Phoenix didn't want to do that, but Sunshine Shores Orchard and Resort had plenty of work trucks he could take. He just didn't want to have a conversation about it with his dad. Then he'd get lectured about buying his own car, and moving back to the family lane, and blah blah blah.

Phoenix didn't need any of his sisters trying to set him up

with their friends. He'd tried that, thank you very much. Gotten engaged. All dressed up for his wedding. And then had his heart shattered in front of all his family and friends, as well as half the town—maybe three-quarters of it—while he stood at the altar and waited for his bride that never came.

Yeah, no thanks.

"Sorry," Jon said, reminding Phoenix that they were still on a call together.

"It's fine, bro," Phoenix said. "Talk to you later." He let Jon end the call while he went back to the hole. It needed to be dug out and reinforced before the post could go back inside. And then he'd probably need more than just the electronic driver he used to get it in deep enough to hold.

So he went back to his lean-to and pulled out the quick concrete, as well as the wire needed to hold the earth out of the way and give the wood something to bite into.

He worked in the silence, something soothing about it that he'd never been able to find anywhere else. He scraped back the leaves and other debris that had blown in there in the few weeks since the post had fallen, then scooped up a shovelful of dirt and tossed it over his shoulder.

"Hey," a woman cried, causing adrenaline to spike inside Phoenix as he spun around.

The blonde woman standing there wore one of those fashionable beanie things on her head, and the hair spilling over her shoulders was so straight that Phoenix thought it unnatural.

"Allegra," he said.

"You threw dirt on me," she said, brushing her leather-gloved hands down her cream-colored coat.

"You're on my property," he said.

"I am not," she snapped back. "I'm clearly still on the state forest side of the line." Her blue eyes flashed fire at him, and dang if Phoenix didn't want to get burned by it. He pulled back the reins of his hormones, because he was definitely not interested in Allegra Wright, senior agent for the Department of Natural Resources.

"And I'm on my side."

"What are you doing?"

"Burying a dead body," he said with a straight face, staring right at her. What did it look like he was doing?

She exhaled heavily like he was the worst man on the planet—which in her eyes, he was—and said, "I've filed another appeal with the Department."

"Good for you," he said. While his stomach twisted the tiniest bit, he had no reason to believe this fourth appeal would go through when the other three had failed. "Did you use that private road again to get out here?" He quirked one eyebrow at her, almost hoping she had. But he'd called the rangers on her last time she'd shown up to inform him she'd filed another appeal, and she hadn't liked that one little bit. But that road wasn't for her personal or professional use, even if she worked for the state. The rangers had told her the same thing he had, but she'd been colder than usual to him after that.

"Of course not," she said. "I had to hike in."

"Shocking." He turned and went back to his work. "You're not going to win. My father planted nineteen trees last spring, and that's well within the guidelines to show improvement on the land." He couldn't understand why the land couldn't just be wild, but Allegra had made it her life's mission to get the piece of land where his cabin sat.

"Hmm," she said, and that only made Phoenix's annoyance increase. He wanted to throw another shovelful of dirt on her, but he twisted slightly so the muck would miss her. Narrowly.

"Hey," she said again.

"Oh, are you still here?" He looked over his shoulder at her, very aware of her presence and knowing exactly where she stood. "What else do you want from me? A kidney?" She'd been badgering him for so long, he sometimes dreamt about her. Or maybe that was because Allegra Wright was incredibly beautiful, and he hadn't dated a single person in five years. Hadn't even been to town in five years.

His cells hummed when she took a step closer. "I was wondering if I could ask you something."

Phoenix narrowed his eyes at her, his mind sifting through what she could possibly ask him. She didn't like him; he didn't like her. They didn't offer advice to each other, other than "I wouldn't cross that line if I were you."

"Another step, and you'll be on my land," he said. "I'm not afraid to call the cops."

"Yeah, I know." She glared at him.

"Rangers aren't cops, sweetheart."

Her eyes practically turned into lasers, and he actually felt a pang of regret hit him. He knew she didn't like being called sweetheart, and yet he couldn't help himself. He really liked seeing her get all hot under the collar, and he while he'd been dealing with Allegra for almost two years and had seen her in spring, summer, fall, and winter attire, he wanted to see what color her shirt was today.

If she'd just take off that coat....

Phoenix derailed his thoughts, because they wouldn't get him anywhere but into a cold shower.

"My brother is coming into town in a couple of weeks," she said through clenched teeth. "He loves birdwatching, and I told him I knew someone who might be able to tell us the best places to go." Her anger faded right before his eyes, and she shook her head. "Forget it. Google knows more than you, I'm sure." She turned and started walking away.

Shock rendered Phoenix silent and still, until he realized she'd just tried to have a real conversation with him. She'd asked him for something that she knew he was good at, liked doing, and had knowledge of.

"Allegra," he called after her, taking a couple of steps and going right over the property line and into the state forest grounds.

She turned halfway back to him and stared up into the trees.

"Try Big Bear Pond," he said. "It's great in the winter, and there's always wildlife there, especially birds."

She gave one single nod, and he felt her slipping away from him again. Which was ridiculous, because he didn't even want her in his life. Right?

He'd chosen the life of woodsman, secluded from everyone on a patch of land surrounded by trees. He'd chosen it for five long years.

"I can get you a guide," he said. "Then he'll know what he's seeing."

Allegra turned fully toward him and advanced like a tiger on the prowl. "That would be great, Phoenix." No thank you, but of course, he hadn't apologized for throwing dirt on her either.

With each inch she came closer to him, Phoenix wondered if it was time for him to choose a different life. One with a certain blonde in it to help keep him warm at night. He licked his lips as she moved to stand right in front of him.

"Anything else?" he practically whispered, his long-dormant hormones refusing to be caged with this woman so close.

"Yeah," she said, stepping her fingers up the zipper of his jacket. "You're on the wrong side of the line, Phoenix. I'm going to call the rangers." And with that, she pulled out her phone, tapped on the screen, and lifted it to her ear.

Ooh, Allegra and Phoenix do NOT like each other...my favorite type of romance!

HIDDEN IN THE WOODS is available now!

BOOKS IN THE FORBIDDEN LAKE SERIES

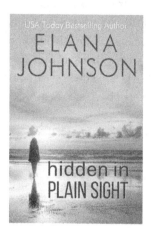

Hidden in Plain Sight (Book 1): He's a member of a prominent family in Forbidden Lake looking to finish his degree. She's trying to make ends meet and stay out of the spotlight, which is pretty much impossible when someone starts a relationship with one of the Addlers...

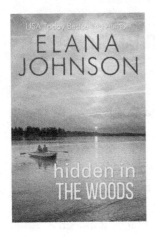

Hidden in the Woods (Book 2): He hasn't left his cabin in the woods in a long time, and he's not keen to give in to the woman who keeps trying to take his land away...until she shows up one night in danger. Can Allegra find a way to take their relationship out of the shadows without putting them both at risk?

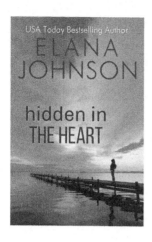

Hidden in the Heart (Book 3): He's a single dad in desperate need of a nanny for the summer. She can provide the help he needs so he can manage the family orchards on the edge of the lake. But can she hold onto her heart, or will she lose it to the man set to take over the Addler empire?

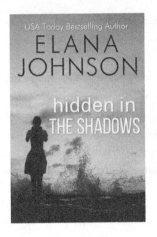

Hidden in the Shadows (Book 4): He owns the biggest business in Forbidden Lake, and his top-floor penthouse overlooks the bay. She's his right-hand in the office...and his biggest crush. Will he tell her the secrets he's never told anyone, or let their chance at love wither away?

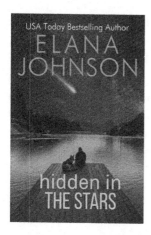

Hidden in the Stars (Book 5): She's the family lawyer and the baby of the Addler family. Her father didn't approve of her last boyfriend, and Mia broke up with the rockstar who'd helped her sister. But he's back in Forbidden Lake, and Mia has some very grown-up decisions to make... Will she admit how she really feels about Declan? Or will her family's wishes win out over her heart?

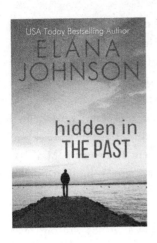

Hidden in the Past (Book 6):
She's a widow raising her baby alone. Even the leader of the motorcycle club knows who Karly Addler is. When he has to walk her down the aisle at her sister's wedding, neither of them expect the attraction between them...

ABOUT ELANA

Elana Johnson is the USA Today bestselling author of dozens of clean and wholesome contemporary romance novels. She lives in Utah, where she mothers two fur babies, works full-time with her husband, and eats a lot of veggies while writing. Find her on her website at elanajohnson.com.